Who's Afraid of the Big Bad . . .

"What's happened?" Nancy asked her friend privately as people shuffled off the bleachers. "Is there anything I can do?"

"Just stick around until everyone else has left, okay?" Brianda asked in a very low voice. Then she continued to help people down from the bleachers and point them to the parking lot.

Nancy, Bess, and George waited for Brianda to rejoin them after every car had pulled away.

Brianda's porcelain skin was flushed a pale pink, and her large blue-gray eyes sparkled with tears in the harsh glow of the security lamp. "It's horrible," she cried. "Khayyam and Liz are not with their pack. Two of our prize alpha wolves—they're *gone*."

Nancy Drew
Mystery Stories

Available from Simon & Schuster

NANCY DREW® 175

WEREWOLF IN A WINTER WONDERLAND

CAROLYN KEENE

Aladdin Paperbacks
New York   London   Toronto   Sydney   Singapore

This book is a work of fiction. Any references to historical events, real people, or real locales are used fictitiously. Other names, characters, places, and incidents are the product of the author's imagination, and any resemblance to actual events or locales or persons, living or dead, is entirely coincidental.

First Aladdin Paperbacks edition November 2003

Copyright © 2003 by Simon & Schuster, Inc.

ALADDIN PAPERBACKS
An imprint of Simon & Schuster
Children's Publishing Division
1230 Avenue of the Americas
New York, NY 10020

Printed in the United States of America

10 9 8 7 6 5 4 3 2

Library of Congress Control Number 2003109058

ISBN 0-689-86182-6

Contents

1

A Wild Night at WildWolf

"It looks like the Holiday Winter Carnival is finally going to get a break from the weather," Nancy Drew said. Light snow dusted the hood of her car as she pulled into Bess Marvin's driveway.

"I know," George Fayne said, reaching to put a new CD into the car's CD player. "At last. We've had nothing but snow, ice, and crispy-cold weather."

Nancy watched Bess pick her way carefully along the icy drive toward the car. Bess was George's cousin, but they looked completely different. George was tall, with short smooth dark hair. Bess was the same age—eighteen—but shorter, and she didn't have nearly as athletic a body as her cousin. Her wavy blond hair was lighter than Nancy's. Bess and

George were not only Nancy's classmates—they were also her best friends.

"Isn't this weather great!" Bess said as she plunked into the backseat. "The Carnival should be spectacular. I can't wait to find out what our work assignments will be!"

"You know, this might be the last Carnival for a while," Nancy said as she turned onto Clayton Avenue. It was the quickest route to Riverside Park, which sat near the Muskoka River. "The last two lost a lot of money."

"Well, the weather was so bad last year, for one thing," Bess pointed out. "Hardly any snow at all. Remember? It was so warm the ice wouldn't hold. And I don't just mean all the sculptures and cool stuff. There was barely enough ice on the Muskoka for skating the full seven days, let alone any real skating competitions."

"The weather wasn't good for a winter carnival, that's true," Nancy said. "But that wasn't the only problem," she reminded them. "Two years ago a lot of money was wasted, and last year half the money disappeared—along with the Carnival chairman. So they've brought in this new guy from Chicago to run things."

"Did you hear his name?" George asked. "It's Poodles McNulty. What kind of a name is Poodles?"

"Especially for a man," Bess said. "It must be some sort of a nickname."

"We might find out this morning," Nancy said, pulling into Riverside Park. Cars already nearly filled the lot. Nancy pulled her Mustang in to join them. The park was sparkling with fresh bright white snow and clear ice.

The three friends gathered up their sports bags and backpacks and got out of the car. Their boots crunched the packed snow as they headed toward the huge blue-and-green tent on the bank of the river. Branches of enormous sycamore trees leaned out across the frozen river near the tent. Maple and oak trees stood straight and tall against the watery-pale sky.

Nancy's new white ski suit showed off her slim body, and she was happy to find out that it also kept her warm and comfortable as they walked through the ice sculpture garden. "Wow, look at these—they're awesome," Nancy said. All around the girls were eight-foot statues of trees, animals, and people carved from ice. Sunshine broke through the sky and glittered through the sculptures.

The girls entered the tent to register for their work assignments. As they stood in line, Nancy recognized many faces—neighbors, friends of her family, shopkeepers around town, and colleagues of her father, attorney Carson Drew.

"There you are." Nancy's boyfriend, Ned Nickerson, strolled toward them. He was taller than Nancy and also had wavy blond hair. He leaned down to give her a kiss, and then gave her friends a warm smile. "Do you have your assignments yet?"

"We just got here," Nancy said, leading the others to a registration line. "What about you?"

"I'm on the team that'll organize the torchlight parades," he answered. "And I'm also going to help with some of the sporting events—the golf tournament and the Polar Bear Plunge."

"Like the Polar Bear Plunge is a *real* sporting event," Bess said. "Give me a break! It's just a group of people in bathing suits jumping through the ice into the river in below-freezing weather."

"I don't know," George said. Her mouth twisted into a crooked smile, as if she still weren't sure about what she was going to say. "I'm thinking about doing it this year."

"Yikes," Bess said. "You would."

"Oh, and get this," Ned added. "I'm one of the judges for the Snow Princess competition."

"That should be right up your alley," Nancy said with a grin.

"Nancy!" a familiar voice called from behind. "It *is* you!"

Nancy turned. "Brianda!" she said. "I haven't seen you since you graduated. Do you all remember each other?" she asked. "This is Brianda Bunch. She was a couple of years ahead of us in school—I knew her when we worked together on the paper. You're in college now, right?" she asked Brianda.

"Yes, finally. My family moved to the West Coast right after I graduated. I worked a year there, and finally started college this past fall—studying journalism at Columbia."

"You must be on school break too," Bess said.

"I am," Brianda answered. "And I came here to hook up with some old friends and get in one more Carnival. It looks like I'm going to be one of the on-call hosts, hanging out to give visitors a quick tour of the Carnival if they want. I'm staying at WildWolf while I'm here."

"WildWolf," Nancy repeated. "That's the animal preserve a few miles out of town, right? We've all been there. It's really cool. Come to think of it, you and I did a feature article on it once. Wait a minute—I remember. Your family's connected to the place . . ."

"That's right," Brianda said. "My cousin is Markie Michaels, the executive director of the preserve. She's an ethologist—a scientist who studies animal behavior. Her specialty is wolves. Hey, would you like to come out tonight? It's Tuesday, so they're having a Howl-o-rama."

"That's when the wolves and the humans howl back and forth?" Bess asked.

"Right," Brianda said. "If you come early I can

5

give you a behind-the-scenes tour. We have some new pups. They're not out for public viewing yet, but I can show them to you. They're incredible."

"I'd love it," Nancy said, "as long as we aren't scheduled to work here tonight."

Bess and George agreed it would be fun. Only Ned begged off. "I can't make it tonight, but I'll take a rain check," he said. "I have to go meet with the torchlighters now, so I'll talk to you later." With that, he bounded off toward a corner of the tent.

Before Brianda left, the others made plans to meet that night at WildWolf. Then Nancy, Bess, and George got their Carnival assignments.

"I'm working at the Heat Hut," Bess said, looking through her orientation kit. "And the cool thing is that I work different shifts every day, so I'll have a good chance of seeing everything before the Carnival is over."

"We'll be able to stay in touch there, too," George pointed out. "The Heat Hut is definitely the place to hang out and get warm—a perfect place for breaks."

"And lattes and hot chocolate and cookies and nachos and all sorts of goodies," Bess added. "What about you, Nancy? Where are you working?"

"I've got several jobs," Nancy said. "You know how they have hosts who stand by to welcome everyone and direct visitors to all the activities and venues?"

"You did that last year, didn't you?" George asked.

"Exactly," Nancy said. "This year I'll be in charge of that team. I make rounds to be sure that all the hosts are on call and helping out, and to see if they have any questions. Oh, and they asked me to be one of the Snow Princess judges, too."

"So you and Ned will be working together for that one," Bess said. "That'll be fun. What are you going to be doing, George?" she asked.

"I'm coordinating the softball-in-the-snow games, and also working with the lighting crew for some of the evening activities," George told them. "I hope I get to work the Crystal Palace for the opening tomorrow."

"That's one of my favorite parts of the Carnival," Nancy said. "That huge ice castle with all the colored lights shining through."

The three split up to meet with their various coordinators and teams for a few hours. As prearranged, they met back at the car at three o'clock. After a late lunch of tacos and burritos at Smoky's Hothouse they headed out to WildWolf.

It was four o'clock and still light when they arrived at the preserve. Nancy pulled off the country road onto a mile-long drive to the gate that opened into WildWolf. They drove another couple of blocks until they came to the visitors' parking lot and a compound of wood-frame buildings. Brianda was waiting for them at the office door. She introduced them to her cousin, Markie Michaels, and Markie's assistant, Christopher Warfield.

"We're so glad you could come," Markie said. She was tall and pretty, with reddish-brown hair.

"Welcome," Christopher added, extending his hand. He had deep green eyes and a British accent. He was stocky, but he looked very muscular.

Brianda immediately took Nancy and her friends to see the wolf pups. The preserve was huge—it was comprised of six four-acre enclosures that were bordered with double security fences. Four to ten wolves lived in each enclosure. WildWolf had an international reputation and was visited by students, scientists, and people from around the world who were interested in animal welfare, nature, education, and research.

Brianda took them into a small building where the wolf babies were being examined by a vet.

"They're so fluffy," Bess exclaimed as she took one in her arms. It looked like a cross between a puppy and a bear cub.

Nancy picked up another wiggly pup with thick brownish fur. It was warm and incredibly soft, and it wriggled up her chest to her shoulder. It nibbled on her hair and murmured baby mumbles in her ear.

"Aren't they amazing?" Brianda said.

"I'm in love," Nancy said, cuddling the pup.

They played with the babies until it was time for

the Howl-o-rama. Then they went back to the first wolf enclosure. It was dark, but a large moon flooded the landscape with a vanilla glow. People started to fill two small bleachers which sat a few yards from the fence—even though a hanging thermometer registered twenty-two degrees.

Markie came out and introduced herself, and said a few words about the preserve and its inhabitants. Then she began the howl. She threw her head back, and a long mournful sound poured from her throat: "*Ah-oooooooooooooooooooooooooooo.*"

From the distance, an echoing call filled the air. Then another wolf from another pen responded, beginning on a different note, so that the two animals howled in harmony.

Markie answered back and motioned for the people in the bleachers to join in. Nancy, Bess, George, and Brianda sent out loud howls and were rewarded with responses from all the packs.

Soon the air filled with an eerie counterpoint of animal and human howling. Nancy's skin sparked with tiny explosions as she sang with the wolves.

During a particularly loud chorus, Nancy noticed a modern sound muted beneath the primitive sound of the howling. She seemed to be the only one who heard the steady rolling crunch of the snow. Suddenly everyone stopped howling and looked toward the new sound. An old pickup truck was shooting toward them along the road that divided two large enclosures.

Christopher Warfield pulled the truck to a grinding halt near the bleachers and hopped out of the truck's cab, leaving the door swinging open. He raced over to the fence where Markie stood. Nancy watched the two of them closely. They were too far away for Nancy to pick up any words from scanning their lips, but there was no question about the news that Christopher had brought. It wasn't good.

"I'm going to see what's going on," Brianda said. She marched down the bleachers, her boots clomping along the wood slats. Brianda joined her cousin and Christopher at the fence, and the three of them huddled for a few minutes. Then Markie and Christopher ran to the truck, and Brianda returned.

"We've had a little problem," Brianda announced to the crowd with a thin smile. "Nothing too bad— but Markie needs to help Christopher clear it up. We're going to cut the Howl-o-rama short this evening. We hope to see everyone back next month. The drive is lit all the way back to the road, so you shouldn't have any trouble finding your way. But be careful—there's ice under all that snow. We don't want any of you sliding into a drift."

Nancy could tell that Brianda was trying to look confident and reassuring—but it was obvious that she was very upset.

10

"What's happened?" Nancy asked her friend privately as people shuffled off the bleachers. "Is there anything I can do?"

"Just stick around until everyone else has left, okay?" Brianda asked in a very low voice. Then she continued to help people down from the bleachers and point them to the parking lot.

Nancy, Bess, and George waited for Brianda to rejoin them after every car had pulled away. Brianda's porcelain skin was flushed a pale pink, and her large blue-gray eyes sparkled with tears in the harsh glow of the security lamp. "It's horrible," she cried. "Khayyam and Liz are not with their pack. Two of our prize alpha wolves—they're *gone*."

2

A Wolf in Sheep's Clothing?

"Gone?" Nancy repeated. "But how? When?"

"I'm not sure," Brianda said. "There's no break in the fence. Somehow, though, they got out."

"You mean . . . *escaped?*" Bess said softly.

"Or were they stolen?" Nancy suggested.

"Without a break in the fence, they couldn't have escaped," Brianda said.

"So if they were taken, it would have to have been by someone who knew this place," Nancy concluded. "And also knew how to handle the animals."

"Khayyam and Liz are alpha wolves—leaders of their pack," Brianda said. "It would not have been easy to capture them."

In the distance Nancy saw snow flying along the

gravel road. The pickup truck and a couple of SUVs raced up. "Looks like they've got everyone in on the search," Brianda said. "They're going to kick you out, too, so I have to make this fast. This isn't—"

"Girls, we're closing up for the evening," Markie called out, interrupting her cousin. "So I'm going to have to ask you to leave. Bree, can you join us in the office, please? Right away."

Nancy waved and smiled. "Bye. The howling was great." She knew it would be better if Markie didn't know that Brianda had told them what happened.

The WildWolf crew went inside the office, and Nancy and her friends started for the parking lot.

In spite of what Markie had said, Brianda escorted them to their car.

"This isn't the first time something bad has happened here," Brianda whispered to the girls. "Markie told me there have been several scary incidents. Personally, I sense that someone is trying to destroy this place and ruin all of Markie's hard work." Nancy could hear the distress in her friend's voice.

"Nancy, I know your reputation," Brianda said. "Help me figure out what's happening here before my cousin loses everything?"

"Of course, Brianda," Nancy said without a moment's hesitation. "I'll look into it and do whatever I can. WildWolf is as of this minute in a sort of lockdown, it seems—outsiders aren't welcome. So listen carefully to everything—take notes if you can. It'll help to have you on the inside. And let's talk tomorrow at the Carnival."

"Thanks, Nancy," Brianda said. "Thanks a lot." She quickly turned and ran back to the office building.

Nancy drove her friends back to town. After dropping Bess and George at their houses, she pulled into her own garage. Nancy sat for a moment in her car, going back over every minute at WildWolf. When she shivered, she told herself it was because it was so cold. But deep down she wondered if it was because there might be two wild wolves on the loose somewhere around River Heights.

At eight o'clock Wednesday morning Nancy's alarm and her bedroom phone both rang at the same time. With one hand she hit the alarm button, and with the other she picked up the receiver.

"Turn on your TV," Brianda said on the other end of the line. Nancy used the remote to turn on her small television set on the bookshelf. The screen showed a local reporter, Susie Oliver, speaking earnestly into a microphone. Nancy caught the point of the broadcast in the middle of the reporter's sentence.

"—standing here in the pasture of local sheep farmer Philip LeRoy, who is understandably concerned about the breaking news we've been bringing to you this morning." The reporter turned to a man who was standing next to her. He looked like he was between fifty and sixty years old—it was hard to tell exactly.

"So, Mr. LeRoy, what was your reaction when you heard that there are two wolves missing from the WildWolf animal preserve, which is not far from here?"

"The same reaction I had the last time it happened," LeRoy said. "I'm mad. Wolves have escaped from that place before, and they attacked my sheep one night about this time of year. I tried to get that place shut down the first time it happened, but nobody'd listen. They'll listen now, I promise you that. WildWolf should be shut down, and all the animals should be destroyed."

"That's outrageous!" someone said out of the camera's range. Nancy recognized the voice, and the camera panned over to Markie's face. "The wolves aren't running loose," she said. "They could not have 'escaped,' as you put it. WildWolf is a supersecure animal preserve, and it meets the strictest federal guidelines for such a facility."

Markie managed a fake smile. "Have you ever visited our preserve, Mr. LeRoy?" she asked. I think your opinion might change if you saw our establishment."

"No, but I don't need to," LeRoy sputtered.

"You *do* admit that two wolves disappeared from WildWolf last night," the reporter said to Markie.

"Yes, but they couldn't have gotten out by themselves," Markie responded.

"Are you saying they're not out there somewhere?" LeRoy demanded. The camera moved so that all three were in view.

"Of course not," Markie said. "But if they are, it's because someone maliciously stole them and *then* turned them loose. Perhaps to cause trouble for WildWolf—to scare everyone who lives around here and to try to shut the preserve down." She gave LeRoy a harsh look.

"Are you accusing *me?*" he yelled. "Are you saying I'd do such a thing? I'll sue you! I want a tape of this program for my lawyer."

The camera zoomed in on the reporter. "As you can see, not only do we have a couple of opinions as to what happened—we also have controversy about *why* it happened. Animal experts from around the state are currently searching for the wolves. Let's hope they find them soon. More news to come on the noon wrap-up. This is Susie Oliver, live from a farm outside River Heights."

"Nancy, I talked to Markie," Brianda said. She was still on the phone. "She'd like to get together with you. She's totally okay with your helping us out. So you can come take a look around any time you want."

Nancy didn't have to report to the Carnival until that afternoon, so she told Brianda she'd be there within the hour. As she pulled on a heavy sweater, Bess called to see whether Nancy had seen the news. Nancy told her about Brianda's call, and Bess agreed to go with Nancy to WildWolf.

They arrived at the preserve five minutes before nine. Markie, Brianda, and Christopher were waiting in the main office building, which was filled with the aromas of warm banana-nut muffins and hot chocolate. They all followed their noses into the conference room and sat around the large table. Brianda and Christopher passed out muffins while Markie spoke.

"People have been trying to shut us down since we opened five years ago," Markie said. "Some people have a basic fear of wolves."

"And that's also one of the reasons WildWolf exists," Christopher pointed out. "So that people can learn more about wolves, see how beautiful they are, and respect them. They're not mean—they're just wild animals."

"Markie has this great reputation all over the world," Brianda chimed in. "She's the one called in to testify in cases involving wolves. She's appeared before a congressional hearing in Washington, D.C. And she was asked to make a speech in London just last month at a big international conference."

"Brianda, thanks for the buildup, but I don't think that's the point here," Markie said.

"Well, I do," Brianda insisted. "I think someone's trying to ruin your reputation by causing trouble at WildWolf."

"That's possible," Christopher added.

"It's not going to work," Markie said. "I'm determined to stand my ground. We're not going down without a fight—and I mean a *fight!*"

"What about the Carnival?" Bess said. "If the wolves are out there running around, do you think they'll head for the Carnival? It would be total chaos if someone saw them there."

"Actually, if they're out there somewhere, they won't go near Riverside Park," Christopher answered. "They're scared of people. There's never been a case in North America of a wild wolf deliberately attacking a person."

"I'd like to take a look at their enclosure," Nancy said.

Christopher, Brianda, and Bess stayed in the office while Markie took Nancy out to the area where the missing wolves lived. The rest of the pack was still there, so Nancy wasn't able to go inside, but she and Markie walked around the double fences. Nancy didn't see any breaks in the wire.

At the part of the enclosure that was the furthest away from the buildings, Nancy saw something on the ground. "What's this?" she wondered aloud. She crouched down to examine a small pile of a grainy, cereal-like mixture. Nearby were two more small piles. She estimated there was maybe a quarter-cup of the mixture in each pile.

"Is this some kind of wolf feed?" she asked.

Markie shook her head. "No," she said. "We don't give the animals anything like that."

"And you don't grow any grains?" Nancy asked.

"We don't grow any crops here at all, except herbs for the kitchen," Markie answered.

Nancy took three pieces of paper from her notebook and fashioned small envelope-type pouches. Then she pinched a sample of the mixture from each pile and dropped them in each of the three envelopes. She placed the packets carefully in the small zipper compartment of her backpack.

Nancy talked to Markie all the way back to the office but didn't learn anything new. As she finally drove back out of the preserve she told Bess about the grainy mixture.

"That's all you found? You don't have a lot to go on so far, do you?" Bess asked, frowning.

"Next to nothing," Nancy said. She stopped at a crossroads and looked at the signs. "That's Norwaldo Road," she read. "They said on the news this morning that that's the road to Philip LeRoy's farm. Let's go pay him a little visit."

19

"Why?" Bess said. "He was mad this morning. He didn't look like someone who welcomes strangers."

"No, but he *did* look like someone who enjoyed telling his story. Maybe he'd like to tell it to a couple of newspaper reporters," she said, smiling.

After a mile of driving Nancy spotted LeRoy's mailbox leaning over the road. She turned into his driveway, which was bordered by pastures. She parked in front of a two-story white house with dark green shutters and took her notebook and pen from her backpack. Then she and Bess trudged toward the house along a rough path dug out of the waist-high snow. Nancy knocked on the door. Within a few moments, it opened.

"Who are you?" Philip LeRoy asked. His face was a rosy red color and his dark eyes pierced into Nancy's.

"I'm Nancy Drew, and this is Bess Marvin. We're reporters for the *River Heights Gazette,* and we're here to get an in-depth story on your feud with Wild-Wolf."

"It's no feud," LeRoy said. "It's a just cause—and it's justice I'm after!"

"Could we have a few minutes?" Nancy asked. "I'm scared of the idea of wolves running loose. I'd like to tell your story. Maybe we can fix this problem so wild animals don't threaten River Heights anymore."

Philip LeRoy blinked, and his expression softened a little. "Come in," he said. "I don't have much time, so please make it quick."

Nancy asked a few questions, repeating several of those that Susie Oliver had asked earlier. LeRoy answered them with the same responses. Then she grilled him about the sheep attacks.

"Exactly when did a wolf attack your flock?" she asked, her pencil ready.

LeRoy stood up and walked behind his chair. "I'm not going into that. My attorney says not to."

"Well, did you see the attacks?" Nancy asked. "How many wolves were there? Are you sure it was wolves and not wild dogs or coyotes?"

"I'm not answering that either," he said, squinting at her. "Say, are you really reporters? You look kinda young to me."

"We're with the student edition," she answered. "I would really like to get an exclusive about the wolves who attacked your sheep."

"I don't think so," he said, walking to the door. "This interview is over."

"Mr. LeRoy—," Nancy began.

"I said it's over! No more questions."

Nancy and Bess hurried out the door and down the path to Nancy's car. In her rearview mirror Nancy could see Philip LeRoy watching her drive away.

"He's scary," Bess said. "I'm glad we left."

As Nancy pulled onto Norwaldo Road, she noticed a service road leading to two large barns far behind LeRoy's house. Trees shielded both sides of the road. "We haven't *quite* left yet," she said.

She drove down the service road and parked the car behind three huge spruce trees so that it couldn't be seen from LeRoy's house. Then she led Bess through the snow to one of the large barns.

"What are we looking for?" Bess whispered, even though there was no one nearby to hear.

"I just want to see the setup," Nancy said. "See where the sheep are kept, see how the wolves might have gotten in. He said on the news this morning that the attack was at night, at this time of year—so the sheep would probably have been in a barn."

Nancy lifted the heavy crossbar and pulled open the barn door. As they went in the door slowly creaked shut behind them. Nancy propped it open with a large rock so that they could have some light.

Even though it was day, the huge room was dark, dingy, and mostly empty. Thin rods of pale sunshine slid through the cracks in the wall and crisscrossed from one side to the other. Gritty dust filled the stripes of light.

"There aren't any sheep in here," Bess said. "There aren't even any animal stalls."

"It's just a storage room," Nancy said. There were

a dozen or so large sealed barrels in one corner. "I think there's a door over there," Nancy said, pointing to the opposite corner.

She walked to a large steel door, pulled it open, and was immediately engulfed in a cloud of frigid cold. "It's a walk-in freezer," she told Bess. "There are more barrels in there."

As she closed the freezer door she heard an ominous scraping noise at the barn door. She turned in time to see a booted foot roll the rock doorstop into the large room. The barn door slammed shut. Nancy raced to the door, but it was too late.

As the crossbar thudded down into its iron cleat, she felt a similar thud in the pit of her stomach.

3

An Unfortunate Meeting

"Nancy, we're locked in!" Bess said.

"He couldn't have seen us drive back here from the house because the trees shielded the road," Nancy said. "He must have followed us."

She looked around the big room. It was even darker now that the door was shut. There were no windows, and even though the room was at least two stories high, there was no loft.

She walked around the room, pushing at wallboards, hoping to find one or two that were loose and could be pushed out enough for the girls to squeeze through. But after a half hour they were no closer to freedom than when the door had slammed shut.

"What are we going to do, Nancy?" Bess asked.

"There's got to be a way out of here," Nancy said.

She paced, her boots shuffling across the dusty wooden floor. "Wait a minute. Remember when we worked at Uncle Bud's pizza place that summer?"

"Yeah," Bess said. "I wish I were there right now instead of trapped in this stinky barn."

"Remember the walk-in freezer?" Nancy asked, walking back to the door in the corner. "Bring that rock that we used for a doorstop over here."

Bess rolled the heavy rock over to Nancy, who was standing in front of LeRoy's walk-in freezer. Nancy continued, "Uncle Bud's walk-in had a back door so they could get deliveries straight from the alley outside."

"I remember that," Bess said.

"Keep your fingers crossed that this walk-in has a back door too." Nancy opened the front freezer door and propped it open with the rock, just in case. Then she walked to the back of the long room. "I've got it," she called back. She tried the door and it opened. "Kick away the rock and come on through."

Nancy heard the other door close with a pneumatic *whoosh*. Bess appeared through the frosty haze, and the two darted out the back door.

They raced to Nancy's car. She didn't admit it to Bess, but she was really relieved to see that the car was still there. Within minutes she was charging down the service road and back out onto Norwaldo Road.

"Look at me, I'm just a mess," Bess said, brushing at her jacket. "I think I have cobwebs in my hair. I need to freshen up before we report for work at the Carnival."

"I need to change clothes too," Nancy agreed, "and I want to make a stop at the chemistry lab at Riverside College. I'm going to drop off the samples of that grainy stuff I found at WildWolf so they can analyze them."

"It's noon now," Bess said, looking at her watch. "Why don't you drop me off at home. I'll drive to the park after I get cleaned up."

"Good idea," Nancy said. "Let's meet up with Poodles McNulty at three."

"Maybe we can find out where he got that name," Bess said with a smile.

Nancy drove Bess home, dropped off the samples at the college, then went to her house. A familiar smell greeted her as soon as she got out of the car.

She followed the delicious aroma into the kitchen. "Hannah," she said, "I could smell your homemade chicken noodle soup clear out in the driveway. The whole neighborhood is going to be lining up for a taste."

"Don't tell your father I made his favorite soup while he was out of town," Hannah Gruen said.

Nancy felt a warm comforting feeling tumble through her—not only from the soup's scent, but also from the familiar sight of Hannah stirring the pot on the stove.

Nancy's mother had died when Nancy was only three years old. Shortly after that, her father had hired Hannah to come live with them. Housekeeper, cook, and loving nurturer for Nancy, Hannah had virtually become part of the Drew family over the years.

"Look at you!" Hannah said, bustling over to pull twigs from Nancy's hood. "Where on Earth have you been? You haven't been out looking for those wolves, have you?" she added with a frown.

"Well, sort of," Nancy admitted, sitting down to a large bowl of soup and some of Hannah's delicious biscuits. While she ate Nancy told Hannah about her activities the previous night and that morning.

"Well, you're old enough—and experienced enough—to know what you're doing," Hannah said. "But you *know* I'll worry about you anyway."

"I'll be careful," Nancy said.

By one twenty Nancy was walking around the Carnival grounds. She was dressed in multiple layers: a thermal unitard, a silk turtleneck, black ski pants, and a long, purple wool sweater. She had slathered plenty of sunscreen on her face and pulled a black-and-white knit hat down over her ears. She was toasty warm even without a coat, although her parka was in the car just in case.

She spent most of the next hour talking to her

team of high-school-student hosts. "Remember, although you're working," she concluded, "we are all encouraged to participate in any of the activities that we choose. For example, I've signed up for the cross-country ski race Thursday night. If you want to participate in any of the sports, feel free to do so."

"That's *any* activity, right?" Brianda asked, walking up to the group. She wore a hot-pink snowsuit that looked really great with her pale skin and dark hair.

"Sure," Nancy said. "It doesn't have to be a sport. If you want to enter the ice-carving competition, grab your chisel or saw and sign up. We have plenty of backup, so we can all enjoy the Carnival. Go look around and I'll see you all at the meeting with Mr. McNulty in half an hour."

Nancy and Brianda went to check on Bess at the Heat Hut. Over choco-lattes Nancy told Brianda about how she'd dropped off the samples at the chem lab.

"And we also paid a visit to Philip LeRoy," Bess added.

"Yes, we pretended we were reporters and asked him a few questions," Nancy said casually, "but he didn't tell us anything he hadn't already said on TV." Then she changed the subject. "Have there been any wolf sightings by the people searching?" she asked.

"Nothing," Brianda said. "No word from anywhere in the state."

At three o'clock Nancy, Bess, and Brianda joined the other workers for a pep rally with the new chairman of the Carnival, Poodles McNulty. The meeting was held next to the Crystal Palace in an outdoor amphitheater, where the Snow Princess would be crowned. The two-story ice castle was draped in black canvas, waiting for the big unveiling later.

The stage was bare when Nancy and her friends took their places on folding chairs. Sun streamed toward them through a pale gray sky streaked with stripes of light blue and peach.

A low rumble of conversation rippled through the air until familiar singsong-y music hushed the crowd. To the accompaniment of "Who's Afraid of the Big, Bad Wolf," a tall, stocky man with a thick cover of spiky red hair loped onto the stage.

He swung his arms as if to conduct the music, and a few people in the crowd sang along.

"Hello, you hardy souls," he bellowed when the song stopped. "Welcome!" He spoke with a lilting accent that Nancy recognized as an Irish brogue.

"Hello!" the crowd boomed back.

"I'm Poodles McNulty, and I'm one hundred percent ready to get this Carnival rockin'. Are you?"

"Yes!" the crowd answered, adding applause and whistles.

"I've heard that some people think wild wolves on the loose is a reason to stop these festivities. Well, they're wrong! We're not going to let a little thing like wolves hanging out in the woods shut us down, are we?"

"No!" There were more cheers and hollers.

"Now, we're not fools," he said, his voice taking on a more serious tone. "We've doubled our security efforts to ensure the safety of our guests—and all of you, of course." His face wound into a huge smile full of sparkling white teeth.

"So relax, and enjoy the extra publicity we're getting because of the two escapees. I've been contacted by national news organizations who are sending journalists here to cover our Carnival. We have those two four-legged rascals to thank for that. So be sure to toast them with some cocoa at the Heat Hut, and have a wonderful time!"

He closed with a reminder about the crowning of the Snow Princess and the Crystal Palace lighting later. Then he asked if there were any questions.

"Where'd you get that name?" boomed a voice from the back of the crowd.

"An excellent question, my friend," McNulty boomed back. "As you can probably tell, I'm Irish," he said, brushing his gloved hand over the top of his auburn spikes. "Before I moved to this country, I was a professional boxer there. The nickname 'Poodles' is a traditional one in Irish sporting circles, and it's

30

stuck with me since my days in the ring. And I want you all to call me 'Poodles,' too. None of that 'Mr. McNulty' stuff, okay?"

Poodles finished by leading a rousing cheer, and then he vaulted off the stage to continued applause. As the crowd began moving out, Ned came up to join Nancy and her friends.

"Well, he's sure getting this party off with a bang," Ned said. He was dressed in a green down ski suit that matched his eyes.

"He sure is. Have you seen George?" Nancy asked.

"I saw her a little while ago," Ned said. "She's working with the crew that will be lighting the Crystal Palace later. If I can get away, let's meet at Smoky's in about a half hour. I'll let George know, too." He waved and hurried off.

Thanks to her orientation training, Nancy was able to give Bess and Brianda a short tour of all the activities and highlights of the Carnival.

"Oh look, a fortune-teller," Bess said, pointing ahead. About a block away a small wooden cabin was painted with brightly colored designs. A neon sign in the shape of a crystal ball glowed above the entrance. "Let's go in."

"Oooh, good idea," Brianda said.

"Okay, let's go," Nancy agreed.

31

When they got inside the cabin, they found that it was empty. The walls were lined with masks, feathers, hats, and bright, exotic clothing. A small heater fanned them with periodic blasts of warm air. "Doesn't look like anyone's here," Bess said. "Hello?"

"I hear something in the back," Nancy said. She started toward the curtains that ran across the back of the small room. Suddenly the curtains parted, and a medium-sized figure stepped through. The person was completely encased in a swirling velvet cape of midnight blue. A full face mask with pale blue lips, a wig, a satin headdress, and gloves completed the outfit. Nancy couldn't tell if the fortune-teller was a man or a woman.

The person motioned for Bess to take a seat on the front side of a small table. The fortune-teller seemed to study Bess's face and palms, and then wrote a note on a piece of paper and folded it into fourths. Handing it over to Bess, the person motioned for her not to open it yet. This routine was repeated with Brianda.

Finally, Nancy took the seat. She stared at the fortune-teller. Nancy had an odd feeling when the person's piercing stare drilled right into her through the tiny eyeholes in the mask. She felt immediately as if she should be on her guard, but she was having a hard time focusing her thoughts. Nancy felt locked into the fortune-teller's gaze. It was almost as if she *couldn't* look away.

A tiny tingling fluttered across the back of her neck as the gloved hand pushed her note across the table. With a wave of its hand, the fortune-teller motioned them out.

Nancy led her friends outside. The sudden shock of cold air seemed to clear her thoughts. She turned to Bess and Brianda. "Okay, let's see what we've got."

"Well, this sure strikes home," Brianda said. "'BEWARE of wolves in sheep's clothing.'" She read the note again and frowned at Nancy.

"Mine is sort of the same idea," Bess said. She smiled faintly, and Nancy could tell she was a little rattled. "'Beware of the bite,'" Bess read. "'It IS worse than the bark.'"

Bess crumpled her note and stuffed it in her pocket. "Well, it looks like the fortune-teller got the cue from Poodles," she said. "Use the missing wolves as a way to punch up the Carnival with extra excitement."

Bess jutted out her chin. Nancy knew that meant her friend was trying to be defiantly brave, even though she was probably a little frightened. "What does yours say, Nancy?" Bess asked.

Nancy unfolded the paper. The tingling at the back of her neck returned as she read. There, in large black letters, was her fortune: BEWARE . . . DANGER.

4

The Message Is Crystal Clear

For a moment she felt like she was back inside the cabin, staring at those eyes behind the mask again. She looked at the fortune again, but her thoughts were interrupted by George's voice.

"*There* you are," George said. "Ned said I should meet you all at Smoky's. So I go, and no one's there. I've been walking all over . . ." She stopped and waved a hand in front of Nancy's shocked face. "Hey, what's the matter with you? Earth to Nancy, Earth to Nancy, come in."

The image of the fortune-teller vanished in a wisp of midnight blue as Nancy shook her head and refocused her thoughts. "Hey, George, I'm glad you could make it. Let's go to Smoky's. I'll tell you all about what happened when we get there."

Ned had already found a table by the time Nancy and her friends arrived. Smoky's had set up a tent in the Park for the Carnival. All the familiar tables, bright tablecloths, and candles were there, along with plenty of tall heaters to keep the customers comfortable. A truck behind the tent, complete with oven and refrigerator, supplied Smoky's famous treats.

Within minutes of taking their seats, Bess and Brianda had shown Ned and George their fortunes and had told them all about the experience.

"Show them what you got, Nancy," Bess urged. "Hers was the scariest one," she told the others.

Nancy unfolded her fortune and pushed it over to George. "This *does* seem a little different," George said. "It doesn't have any cutesy references to wolves in it. It looks like it's really serious—not a joke."

"I agree," Brianda said, rereading the words. "Nancy, yours is sort of . . . more personal."

"I'm feeling kind of weird," Bess said in a hushed voice. "If it *is* personal . . . what if that fortune-teller can really see into the future? What if it's true?"

Nancy agreed that her fortune seemed different than the others. It had given her an odd feeling, too. But she could tell that Bess and Brianda were beginning to get worried, so she decided to play it cool until she was completely sure.

"Don't forget," she pointed out, "the fortune-teller is a paid entertainer. Everyone's talking about the missing wolves right now."

"Poodles is encouraging it," Ned reminded them. "He thinks it's good for business."

"Exactly," Nancy said. "The fortune-teller surely picked up on that. Everyone's probably going to get scary fortunes, and ones that have a wolf-like theme. It's all a gimmick to flood the Carnival with mystery and excitement."

"Yeah, but yours was different," Brianda said. "The message—"

"Food's here," Nancy interrupted, relieved to see the platters heading toward their table. She had decided a change of subject was just what the party needed.

"Guess what," George said, dipping her burrito in salsa. "I'm going to be helping with the lights for the unveiling of the Crystal Palace."

"So we heard," Nancy said. "I know you really wanted to be in on that."

"It's *so* cool," George explained. Her dark eyes glinted with reflections from the heater near their table. "It's going to be the most spectacular setup ever. We rehearsed for hours this afternoon."

"Have you seen the palace and everything?" Bess asked.

"It's really something," George said with a nod.

"Huge—two stories high. And parts of it have been hollowed out, so we can get in there and set up lights. There are lots of towers and windows and decorations cut out around the top."

"And all carved from ice," Brianda said. "I'm always stunned by what they can do."

"With a lot of hard work and a dozen chainsaws," Ned added.

"When the name of the Snow Princess is announced," George told them, "they're going to turn out all the other lights in the area—that's new this year. Then the drapes will fall away and we'll flip the switches. Thousands of lights will go on inside the Palace, and all these different colors are going to shoot out through the ice walls. It'll be amazing."

"I think this will be the best Carnival ever," Bess said. Nancy was relieved that her friend seemed to be over her jitters from the fortunes they'd gotten earlier.

After lunch Nancy and her friends took off to perform their various duties. Bess headed to the Heat Hut, and George went to the Crystal Palace. Ned left to meet with the torchlight parade committee, saying he would see Nancy at the Snow Princess judges' table.

The Carnival opened at dusk to a huge crowd. Nancy and Brianda walked to the park's entrance where the other members of Nancy's team of hosts were gathered. Nancy watched while her team passed out maps and offered to direct visitors or to escort them to different activities and events.

Finally Nancy reported to the outdoor stage. Huge heaters perched atop poles radiated warmth onto the stage and into the audience. In front of the first row of seats was a long table. Nancy took her seat at the table with the other Snow Princess judges. Ned was already there, and he introduced Nancy to Susie Oliver, the local television reporter she had watched that morning. Susie was going to be the emcee for the competition.

"I saw your interview with Philip LeRoy and Markie Michaels," Nancy said to Susie. "So what did you think? Was Mr. LeRoy telling the truth? Or is he just trying to get WildWolf shut down?"

"You know, I can't decide," Susie said. "They both seemed to make sense to me. Frankly, I don't care who's right as long as those wolves get back where they belong. I really don't like the idea of those beasts running around the woods."

"I don't think you really have to worry," one of the other judges said. Ned introduced him as Jax Dashell, detective with the River Heights police force. "I'm on special assignment, heading up the Carnival security detail," he explained.

"And you don't think we have to worry about the missing wolves?" Susie asked. She was even prettier in person than she was on television. About thirty years old and shorter than Nancy, she had short, spiky, nearly white hair.

"No," Detective Dashell said. "Wolves are frightened of people. They like to keep what the animal handlers call a long flight distance between themselves and human beings."

"Has it occurred to any of you that we've got more than a wolf problem on our hands?" said the last judge at the table.

"Willy, I already know what you're going to say," Detective Dashell said.

"Nancy, this is Willy Dean," Ned said. "He owns a mailing service. Willy has an interesting twist on the wolf story."

"Okay, okay, don't believe me," Willy said. "But I tell you I've seen it, and it's no joke." Willy was average looking—brown hair, brown eyes. But he had muscular arms and shoulders, as if he did serious weight training.

The music started, announcing the beginning of the Snow Princess parade.

"Seen what?" Nancy asked, leaning closer so she could hear Willy over the music.

"The werewolf," Willy answered, opening his judging book to the first page. "You know, one of those creatures that's a regular person in the daytime, but turns into a wolf when the moon is full. I've seen one running around here lately."

The lively music cut off Nancy's startling conversation with Willy and heralded the parade of finalists for the honor of being crowned Snow Princess. Each finalist had already performed in a talent competition and had been interviewed by the Carnival committee. Tonight they were appearing in ballgowns on the heated stage. The judges were to evaluate them on poise and appearance. These points would be combined with totals from the other two competitions to determine this year's Snow Princess.

Susie introduced five women who walked across the stage in gorgeous white gowns. Some of the dresses were plain but very elegant. Others were glitzier, decorated with lace or beads.

Without talking, the judges recorded their votes. Susie collected them, and she, Poodles, and a couple of other people huddled around a computer, adding up the totals.

Susie then went back to the microphone with a note in her hand. "Ladies and gentlemen," she announced. A low drum roll stuttered from the back of the stage. "The Carnival committee and I are proud to introduce you to this year's River Heights Holiday Winter Carnival Snow Princess . . . Miss Julie Taylor!"

The women on the stage all gasped and clustered around the new Snow Princess. Susie placed a rhinestone tiara on her head, and the Snow Princess was led by Poodles to the canvas which had been draped around the Crystal Palace. She and Poodles grasped the cord that would bring down the curtain.

All the lights around the area dimmed and then blacked out, as George had predicted. Everyone waited a moment in the dark, staring at the drape. Nancy held her breath as the drum roll grew louder, more urgent.

Finally the Snow Princess pulled the cord and the canvas shroud dropped from the Crystal Palace. Lights burst on with an elegant fanfare.

But only one color—blood red—spiked through the ice. And it shone through large block letters carved into the wall, letters that warned: BEWARE . . . DANGER.

5

Who's Afraid of the Big Bad Wolf?

A weird sound—a sort of collective gasp—rustled through the crowd. Nancy felt her skin ripple in response. A few startled screams punctuated the last gasp.

As Nancy stared at the blood-red words glowing on the wall of the Crystal Palace, she reached into her pocket and wrapped her hand around the fortune.

"Nancy," Bess whispered next to her. "That's your fortune. It's the same message!"

Nancy clenched the paper until her fingers started to hurt. Then she shook off the anxious chill and stood up. Instantly, everyone moved into action. Some people scurried away. Others pointed with tentative, nervous-sounding laughs.

"Raise the drapes," Poodles McNulty yelled. "Get those drapes back up." A few members of the production crew began reattaching the black canvas drape to the metal ring. Then they hoisted it into place, masking the ice building from view again.

Nancy raced to the large lighting booth to find George, and Ned followed close behind. George was working frantically with the rest of the technicians.

"Tell me it was a joke," Nancy said, "or some crazy scheme cooked up by Poodles McNulty."

"I don't know," George said. "We're shocked too. We're trying to put the pieces together now."

"Okay," boomed Poodles, rushing in. "You had your fun and stirred up the crowd. Whoever did it gets a gold star for ingenuity and marketing. Which one was it?" He looked at each of the lighting technicians with a tight smile. He acted as if he was okay with what happened. But Nancy could tell he was simmering beneath that smile.

"Don't worry—I'm not firing anyone," Poodles said. "It was just a prank—I know that." He looked into each person's face. When he got to Nancy's, he seemed to study hers longer than the others.

"No one's taking the credit?" Poodles asked, pausing for a moment. "Okay—just get the original lighting plan back in place. No one leaves until it's done." Then he charged back out of the room.

"Boy, he really gave you a once-over," Ned said to Nancy.

"He was probably trying to figure out who she is and what she's doing here," George offered.

Nancy smiled and nodded at her friends. *Was that it?* she wondered. *Or was it something else?*

"I have to get to work," George said. "We have to reprogram everything." She lowered her voice. "I'll let you know what we find out," she promised Nancy.

"Let's go," Nancy said to Ned. "I want to see something." Nancy and Ned left the lighting booth and went behind the curved wall—the "shell"—that formed the back of the amphitheater. When they got to the edge of the shell they could see the draped Crystal Palace next door.

Nancy stopped Ned and they ducked into the curved shadow that the shell cast across the snow. The wind had picked up a little. The drapery surrounding the Palace rippled as the wind blew across it. Every few seconds a gust would hit the opening where the two ends of the drapery came together. The black canvas would lift up slightly and blow away, revealing the ice building inside.

"There's Jax Dashell," Nancy pointed out. The detective was standing nearby. "He must be guarding the Palace. I need to get past him. If you can get him away from his post for a few minutes, I can sneak through the opening in the drape."

"I'm on it," Ned said. He hurried out from behind the shell and up to Detective Dashell.

Some of their conversation traveled to Nancy's ear on the dry, cold air. First she heard words like "shock," "Willy," "werewolf," and "panic." Then Ned pointed toward the stage. "Come on," he said, loud enough for Nancy to hear. "You'd better talk to them. You can still see the Palace from there."

Ned led Detective Dashell away and toward the stage. As they passed by Nancy, hiding in the shadows, she held her breath. Then, while they climbed the steps to the stage, she darted inside the drapes to the Palace, pulling the ends of the cloth together behind her.

Even in the darkness the Crystal Palace glistened. Someone had set up a couple of portable worklights on poles. They weren't very bright, but the dim bulbs caused a dramatic effect. The lightbeams shot around and through the ice, forming sparkling patterns on top of patterns.

Nancy hurried right to the wall where the threatening words had appeared. She examined the carving. From the gouges and pointed holes she figured that the letters were hammered out with a chisel rather than cut with a chainsaw.

She turned on her penlight so she could pinpoint the area around the carving. Her eyes narrowed as she concentrated. She didn't want to miss anything.

And she knew she didn't have much time before Detective Dashell returned to his post.

She scanned the ground carefully. Suddenly her breath caught in her throat. An icy breeze wafted by. Something fluttered in the dark shadows near the floor. She crouched and pinned the area in her pen-light beam. Several small, purple twists of silk stuck to the wall of ice.

As she stared at the fluttering fabric her mind flashed back to a colorful picture. She was in the fortune-teller's cabin at the moment its host swept in—and the fortune-teller had been wearing a cape bordered with purple fringe.

Her heart stepped up a few beats and she pock-eted two of the purple fragments, leaving the other pieces for subsequent evidence-gatherers. Then she ducked out of the Palace without being seen. Cir-cling around the amphitheater shell, she headed straight for the fortune-teller's cabin.

She stepped inside the painted building. "Wel-come, Miss," a friendly elderly woman said. She had grayish hair and wore a filmy, bright-colored dress layered over a tunic. Chandelier earrings trailed down and rested on her shoulders.

"We've had strange things happening this evening," she continued. "Would you like to know what it means for you? Show me your palm and I'll tell you." She smiled warmly.

"Actually, I wanted to speak to the other fortune-teller," Nancy said.

"But there is no other one," the woman explained. "I am the only fortune-teller."

"There was someone here earlier," Nancy said. "With a mask and a cape." Nancy looked around.

"A white mask with pale blue lips?" the woman asked. She looked at the back corner of the room. Nancy followed her gaze to see a couple of bare nails poking out of the wall. "I wondered where it went. Was the cape dark blue, by any chance?"

"With purple fringe," Nancy added with a nod.

"Oh boy," the woman said. She dropped her dramatic, mystical air and talked like a real person. "I just got here. I was called away earlier on an emergency. Thank goodness it turned out to be a false alarm. I'm still feeling a little rattled."

"That must have been really scary," Nancy said. "Who called you about it—the police?"

"I don't know who it was," the woman admitted. "Some guy raced in the back door saying the Carnival office got a call that my house was on fire and I had to get right home. I just panicked and ran. I didn't stop to ask any questions."

"And you don't know who called?" Nancy asked.

"No," the woman said. "I just figured it was a neighbor. But when I got home, everything was fine."

"Can you describe the man who raced in with the message?"

The woman thought for a moment, then shrugged her shoulders. "No. I can't picture him at all. I was just so scared. Hey, do you think he's the one who stole my costume? Seems like a lot of trouble to go to for just an old cape and mask." She paused for a moment. "Why are you asking all these questions, anyway?"

"Just curious. I'm glad it was a false alarm."

"Me too. I don't like the idea of someone ripping me off like that, though. Thanks for helping me figure everything out. How about letting me read your palm? No charge, of course."

"I'll have to take a rain check on the fortune," Nancy said, smiling. "See you later."

Nancy ducked out of the cabin and went back to the amphitheater.

"I couldn't find you," Ned said. He sounded worried. "Did you hear me earlier? I made up a story about Willy revving up a group backstage with talk about a werewolf," he said proudly. "Then I asked Jax to calm the crowd down before anyone panicked."

"I heard parts of that," Nancy said. "Good job—it worked."

"For a little while, anyway," Ned said. "We looked around, and of course Willy and the group weren't there. Finally he decided they had all left. By the time we got back to the Palace, you were gone."

Nancy told him what she'd found stuck to the Palace. Then she described her meeting with the *real* fortune-teller.

"Nancy, I don't get this," Ned said. "You're saying that the person who gave you, Bess, and Brianda your fortunes was a fraud?" Ned stared at the snow for a minute. "Wait a minute," he continued. "That means the fake one was there *specifically* to give you those fortunes!"

"It could be," Nancy said. "So far, I can't figure out any other reason for the whole charade."

"So the fake fortune-teller was targeting you," Ned said again. "But how would the person even know you were going there? That doesn't make sense."

"How about this," Nancy suggested. "Someone is following us. Maybe it's the person who stole or released the WildWolf animals. He's not *planning* to do the fortune-telling bit. He's just keeping tabs on us. But then he hears us talk about getting our fortunes told, and he sees an opportunity to scare us. So he runs around to the back of the fortune-telling cabin."

"He tells the real fortune-teller that she's got an emergency at home, to get her out of the way," Ned added.

"Right," Nancy agreed. "She rushes away, and he looks around and sees the costumes. Maybe he's even been in the cabin before, so he knows there are disguises available. He pulls on the mask, gloves, and cape, and waits in the back of the room."

"Knowing you three are on your way," Ned finished.

"Exactly," Nancy said. "He hands us the fortunes and clears out as soon as we leave."

"So you think he's got something to do with the wolfnapping, and knows you're on the case?" Ned asked.

"What I know for sure is this: Someone who didn't belong in the cabin was in disguise, handing us fortunes. Why? And it also seems like more than a coincidence that my fortune was exactly the same as the message in the Crystal Palace wall."

"So the fake fortune-teller was the same person who carved the nasty message in the ice," Ned concluded.

"Maybe," Nancy said. "If so, he's smart—the kind of person who sees an opportunity and goes for it."

"Well, just the idea of someone following you in the first place bothers me," Ned said.

"I'm totally with you on that one," Nancy said. "So we need to find out if our assumptions are true, and if so, who this impostor is, and why he—or she—is doing all this."

Ned looked at his watch. "Okay, I'm in trouble," he said.

"I thought I heard the band tuning up," Nancy said. "It must be time for the torchlight parade."

"Yep—and I'm supposed to help get it started. Let's meet at the Heat Hut after, okay?"

"I'll be there," Nancy assured him.

"Be careful!" Ned called back.

Nancy quickly checked on her team, but it really wasn't necessary. Everyone was lining up for the torchlight parade.

At last she made it back to the Palace area, where Detective Dashell was still manning his post. She told him about the bogus fortunes she and her friends had gotten from the fake fortune-teller. She even confessed to sneaking into the Palace and finding the fringe in the ice. He nodded as she talked, but his smoky blue eyes narrowed when she told him about her conversation with the true fortune-teller.

"Okay, I've heard enough to tell you that I want you to back off, Nancy," Detective Dashell said. His face had a kindly expression, but his voice was stern, and she could tell he meant what he said.

"If you're being followed and threatened," he said, "it's time for us to step in. I've been on the police force for a few years, so I'm aware of your skill in solving cases. But we can't have you putting yourself in danger. I'll follow up with the fortune-teller and try to track down the fake one."

"Will you tell me if you find out anything?" Nancy asked.

"If it will keep you off the trail, yes."

"Deal," Nancy said. She left to pick up Bess for the parade.

It began with a few men wielding flaming torches as they walked to the river. Behind them, white horses pulled carriages which carried the Snow Princess and her court. Costumed figures were next—Jack Frost, winter elves, and the cast of the ballet company's production of *The Nutcracker*.

Poodles McNulty began a group sing of "Winter Wonderland," and the spectators chimed in. Laughing and singing, Nancy and Bess joined Ned at the end of the parade.

As they neared the river the music wound down. Before another song could begin, a new sound floated along the river and filled the ears of the paraders. It was the same eerie wail that had chilled the blood of humans for centuries. The howl of a lone wolf rose and fell through the thin air.

Nancy turned to find the source of the sound. Everyone around her followed her lead. There, on a bridge spanning the Muskoka, they saw the silhouette of a wolf sitting on its haunches. As they watched, it leaned its head back and pointed its long, tapered nose toward the sky. Another mournful cry left its throat and filled the air.

While a third howl poured out from its lungs, the beast rose up on its back legs, standing tall in the moonlight.

6

The Hair of the Wolf

This time the crowd's reaction was stunned silence. Everyone stood still and stared. There was no collective .gasp—not even any screams. Some people seemed to be holding their breath.

Nancy was *not* holding her breath. In fact, it was coming pretty fast—faster than comfortable. She couldn't take her eyes off the figure on the bridge. It almost seemed as if none of this was real. People carrying torches, a werewolf howling in the moonlight . . . it was like watching an old horror movie, except she wasn't in her comfy house with a big bowl of popcorn in her lap. She was outdoors in the bitter cold, mixed signals rushing through her brain.

The beast on the bridge let out one more bone-chilling howl before loping off on two legs into the shadows on the opposite bank of the river. By the time the air was quiet again the wolf had disappeared into Ripple Woods.

The silence continued for a moment or two. It was suddenly broken by a smattering of applause. Everyone was wearing gloves, so the claps were muffled, but the sound grew and was soon accompanied by full-fledged cheers.

"It was an actor," Bess said, letting out a large sigh. "Of course—it *had* to be."

"I guess so," Ned concluded. "Just part of the whole opening night festivities. Poodles is really trying to spin this thing positively, that's for sure."

"I can see everyone thinks it's part of the show," Willy said out loud. "You all figure that was just entertainment for the Carnival. But I'm telling you, I've seen that creature before. He was slinking across a field. Now you tell *me* how that wolf's got anything to do with the Carnival!"

Willy walked off, mumbling to himself.

The torchlight parade ended at the riverbank. The *Nutcracker* cast performed a few highlights of the ballet on the hard ground, and the crowd dispersed pretty quickly after that.

Everyone was buzzing about the scary message in the Crystal Palace wall and the werewolf on the bridge. Most people seemed to think the performance was part of the fun, but Nancy picked up a nervous jitter underlying all the excitement. Carnivalgoers walked quickly to their cars and sped from the parking lots out into the wintry night.

Nancy's friends had chores to complete before leaving their jobs for the evening. She checked all her hosts out for the evening, answered a few questions about the next day's schedule, and finally headed for home.

"Wow, does this feel good," she said out loud, finally sinking down into her bed. Although the thermostat was set the same as it always was this time of year, she just couldn't seem to get warm. She pulled the covers close up around her face, but sleep didn't come easily. She thought back over the day—from being locked in Philip LeRoy's barn to the crazy evening at the Carnival.

She couldn't chase from her mind the figure covered in wolf hair standing on the bridge until a veil of sleep finally draped over her brain.

For the second morning in a row, a ringing phone jarred Nancy awake.

"Hi, it's me." This time it was Bess's familiar voice. "Has Brianda called you yet?"

"No," Nancy answered, sitting up and yawning. "What's up?"

"She and I talked last night before we went home. We both have late shifts today," Bess explained, "and we thought we'd see if there's anything that we can do to help on the case this morning. Maybe there's some lead you want us to follow up on?"

"Hey, thanks," Nancy said. "Actually, I'm not going in until this afternoon myself. I was going to call the chemist and see if he knows what that stuff was that I found near the wolf enclosure. Markie couldn't identify it, so it must be something brought in from outside."

"Do you want me to call?" Bess offered.

"I'll do it," Nancy answered. "But stand by. After I talk to him let's have breakfast, and we'll go from there. Want to call Brianda and ask her to come too?"

Bess hung up, and Nancy took a shower. She pulled on jeans and a heavy white cable-knit sweater. After chugging a glass of juice she called the college and talked to the chemist. Then she called Bess back. Brianda had just arrived at Bess's house. Nancy told them to meet her at Net 'n Nosh computer café. "Bring your laptop," she told Bess.

Within fifteen minutes they were all seated at a window table. It was perfect weather—not as cold as the day before, but way too cold for the ice to melt. The sunlight bathed everything in a bright glow.

"George is already working," Bess told Nancy and Brianda as they ordered their breakfasts. "They're still trying to get all the schematics restored for the lighting program. Someone really hacked away at it to get the red lights shining perfectly through that scary message."

"I haven't heard from Ned this morning," Nancy said. "He's probably already on the job too. I'd really like to talk to George, so I'm thinking about going over to the Carnival early."

"Did you talk to your chemist friend?" Brianda asked, sipping her foamy latte.

"I sure did—and guess what? That substance I found is a homemade animal feed. It's fifty percent standard grains, plus some other grasses and herbs that would appeal to *sheep*."

"Sheep!" Brianda said, her upper lip fluffy with frothy cream.

"Exactly," Nancy confirmed. "That's why I had you bring your computer, Bess. See what you can find on Philip LeRoy. I know he's been interviewed for the newspaper as well as television. Those interviews will be in the archives somewhere—you can start there. Get me anything you can find out about him."

The waitress brought breakfast. Brianda had ordered French toast, Bess a Belgian waffle, and Nancy a vegetable omelet.

"That might take a while," Bess said, pouring blueberry syrup over her waffle. "There are lots of sites I can check."

"Whatever you can find out will be great," Nancy said.

She told Bess and Brianda about her meeting with the real fortune-teller. Both girls were visibly distressed by that news. The three talked over the theory Nancy had about being followed and fooled by the fake fortune-teller.

"I don't like being followed," Bess said, looking out the window. "It's not the first time—but that doesn't make it any easier."

"I told Detective Dashell what happened, so I'm sure he's looking into it. But Brianda, while Bess is tracking down info on LeRoy, I'd like you to check back with the real fortune-teller. Find out whether she's remembered anything more about the man who got rid of her so he could take her place."

"Okay. So what did you two think of the werewolf?" Brianda asked.

"Everyone seems to think it's part of the fun," Bess offered. "I'm hoping they're right."

"That's what I've heard, too," Brianda said. "I mean, there are no real werewolves, right? I just hope it's not someone trying to scare people about our missing wolves. Markie's so afraid Khayyam and Liz will get hurt, or worse, if they're out there just running around and some nutcase sees them."

"Let's get to work and make sure that doesn't happen," Nancy said. "Let's find the wolves first."

They quickly finished breakfast and went to the Carnival. It was a few minutes past ten. Brianda left immediately for the fortune-teller's cabin. Bess took her computer to the Heat Hut, where she could work at a table in the back until her shift started.

The temperature had dropped ten degrees, so Nancy pulled on a pair of blue snow pants that she'd brought. With those and her hooded parka she knew she could handle the frigid air.

Her first stop was the lighting booth at the amphitheater. George welcomed the break. "We still don't know who did it," she said. "The lighting schematic was computer-driven, so the person probably knew theater lighting. Sabotaging the original program and substituting another is pretty standard tech stuff. Speaking of techies," George said, looking over Nancy's shoulder.

Nancy turned around and saw Bess scampering across the icy ground toward them. "I've got to go to work in a few," Bess said. "But I wanted you to have what I found so far. I went back to the computer café to print out a couple of articles that LeRoy wrote for livestock magazines."

"Look at this," Nancy said, scanning the sheets. "It seems that Mr. LeRoy customizes his winter feed for the flock."

"He includes a few recipes there," Bess added. "He even has his own web page, and he sells packages of his grain concoction to people all over the world."

"I'll bet that's what was in those barrels in his barn," Nancy said. "Bess, this is excellent."

"I'll search some more on my breaks," Bess said. "Come by later! See ya." With a broad grin she went back to the Heat Hut.

Nancy had an hour left before she reported for duty. She strolled over to the fortune-teller's cabin, but there was a line outside. She didn't see Brianda, so she walked on. She kept an eye out for Detective Dashell, but didn't see him either. Nancy ended up at the field next to the park where a rousing softball-in-the-snow game had started.

Nancy stopped for a while and watched the game. When the inning was over and the teams changed sides she saw Philip LeRoy stride toward second base.

"Well now," Nancy mumbled. She walked to the parking lot near the softball field. She recognized the truck parked at the end of the lot as the one she'd seen in LeRoy's drive.

Nancy looked around. The lot was empty. Everyone was on or near the softball field, playing or cheering. Nancy walked casually to LeRoy's truck and peered into the empty truck bed. It looked clean, but she knew that you don't always see everything in the first glance.

It took about five minutes to finally spot what she'd hoped to find: a few small piles of a grainy mixture like the one she'd found at WildWolf. She gathered some up, leaving the rest where it was. She put a couple of tablespoons of the mixture into an empty film canister she had in the small sports pack strapped around her waist.

She then crouched and checked all the tires. The first two were packed with snow and a few twigs and leaves in the tirewells. Then she saw something dark buried in the snow behind one of the wheels. She flashed her penlight into the tirewell. Her pulse skipped so rapidly that she felt a tingling on the sides of her neck. A sudden shiver made the penlight beam bobble up and down.

She stripped off the glove of her right hand and reached into the packed snow on LeRoy's truck. She hardly felt the cold on her fingers as she pulled away a clump of gray-white hair with dark brown tips.

Nancy folded the hair into a tissue and stuffed it into her bag. Then she stood up and went back over the truck bed, inch by inch. She found a couple more large hunks of the hair jammed under a flap in the corner of the truck bed. She put the smallest hunk in her bag and left the other, folding the rubber flap back down over it.

Her heart was still pounding. *Get a grip,* she told herself. *That could be cat hair or dog hair. There are lots of animals on his farm from which this hair might have come.*

61

She walked quickly back into the Carnival grounds. "But it could be wolf," she muttered. "Markie will know for sure. And if it is . . ."

Nancy stopped at the Heat Hut for a mocha latte. Bess was too busy to talk, but she gestured that she'd meet Nancy at three o'clock. Nancy checked in for work and began making her rounds, talking to her team of hosts.

She came across Brianda at the two-story snow slide near the south end of the park. For a week, carpenters and other Carnival workers had constructed the manmade hill. They had packed snow onto a carefully engineered scaffolding, building it up until it was a superslide. Every year this was one of the Carnival events that drew the biggest crowd—especially among River Heights teens.

This Thursday afternoon was no exception. Nancy and Brianda sat on a nearby bench and watched the fun. The slide was already superslick from all the people who had used it. The frozen snow was polished to a high shine.

Dozens of people patiently climbed the stairway, one slow step at a time, while those at the top prepared to skid to the bottom.

Nancy unzipped her sports pack. "I want to show you something," she told Brianda. "I found—"

Her words caught in her throat when she heard the first crunch. It wasn't the soft crunch of snow. It was another sound—brittle and snaplike. Nancy knew it was a sound that didn't belong with the snowslide.

Then she heard a loud *craaaaaaack*. The sun was so bright on the two-story pile of snow that when she saw the hill seem to shudder, she hoped it was a mirage. But it wasn't her imagination. As if it were experiencing a mini-earthquake, the two-story snowslide shivered again, then convulsed into a small avalanche. Sliders and climbers tumbled down in a booming tidal wave of snow and ice.

7

A Fortune Comes True

Nancy's latte dropped in a splash of coffee and white chocolate, staining her blue snow pants and the snow at her feet. She raced to what had been the foot of the slide. It was now a jumble of snow, hats, boots, ice, and people.

She heard several people calling for help, so she dug right in, pawing with her hands to free people from the globs of snow and ice. Brianda followed her lead. Others joined them, and Ned and Willy soon showed up to help as well.

"I suppose you all think this was an accident," Willy muttered. "I'm telling you it's not. It's more of the curse of the werewolf, and that's the truth."

"Not now, Willy," Ned said. "Let's just work at getting these people out of here."

"Not now, Willy . . . not now, Willy. That's all anyone ever says to me. I can't get security to listen, I can't get the police to listen. *Somebody's* got to find that beast and stop him or this Carnival's going to fall apart just like this snowslide."

Jax Dashell and Poodles McNulty arrived within seconds of each other. A few doctors jumped in to set up a triage in the snow. They checked all the injured and ranked them as to how seriously they were hurt. When the emergency crews arrived with their ambulances—which happened quickly—the ones with the worst injuries went to the hospital first.

Detective Dashell and other security officers took charge of the rescue effort, pitching in to get everyone free. Poodles supervised the maintenance workers who arrived with hand shovels, snowblowers, and small trucks with digging equipment.

It took over two hours to rescue everyone. By the time the last person was pulled out of the avalanche, Nancy's arms and shoulders ached and she was emotionally drained. Many of the people caught in the avalanche were her friends or others she knew at school. Finally, she, Ned, and Brianda sank down onto a bench.

Nancy couldn't help remembering a few hours earlier when she had sat on the same bench to enjoy her latte and watch the fun.

Brianda checked her watch. "Nancy, my shift is

almost up. If it's okay with you, I'd like to get back to WildWolf. Markie's probably heard about this by now, and she'll be worried."

"No problem," Nancy said. She remembered the wolf hair in her pack that she had found on Philip LeRoy's truck. "I need to talk to her again," she told Brianda. "Have her give me a call."

As Brianda walked off, Jax Dashell dropped onto the bench next to Nancy and Ned. "Thanks for all your help," he said, looking around. "What a mess!"

Nancy followed his gaze. There was still a three-inch glaze of snow on the slide itself, and a pile left at the top. Here and there she could see part of the wood scaffolding—the base structure—peeking through the icy snow that was left.

But at the bottom of the slide there were piles everywhere, still littered with hats and boots and gloves. When it came down, the avalanche had rolled along the street at the bottom of the slide, picking up people, trash cans, a cart selling roasted chestnuts, and everything else in its path. Then it had tossed them several yards away. Police had roped off a wide area with yellow "Do Not Cross" tape.

"Did we really get all the people out of there?" Nancy asked. "Is everyone accounted for?"

"Thankfully, yes," Detective Dashell answered. "And there were no critical injuries—nothing life-threatening. Broken bones, and some pretty bad sprains. And there were a few that looked okay, but the medics still thought they needed some X rays. They've all been taken to medical centers. The rest—the ones with minor cuts and scrapes—are being treated in the extra ambulances. It's a miracle it wasn't worse."

"It was bad enough," Ned murmured, shaking his head.

"Well, I'm going to talk to some of the people being treated here," Detective Dashell said, "and see if they can tell me anything about what happened." He smiled at Nancy and Ned and then left.

"That's just what I was thinking of doing," Nancy told Ned. "I'm going to walk around this area and talk to some of the witnesses."

"You're not starting to think like Willy, I hope," Ned said. "Are you saying this might not have been an accident?"

"There's only one way to find out," Nancy said, "and that's to start asking questions."

When she stood up she saw George rushing down the street toward the scene. Nancy hurried over to the temporary border of yellow police tape. She introduced herself to the police guard posted there. "You probably saw me talking with Detective Dashell on that bench," she said in a very businesslike manner, pointing back at the area around the slide.

The guard nodded slightly. "Well, this is George

Fayne," she said quickly. "She's here to help us with the investigation."

Without waiting for a response Nancy turned to George, saying, "We've been waiting for you. Jax is in the ambulance." Then she pulled the tape up out of the way and ushered George into the confined area. They jogged away from the guard without looking back—and without being stopped.

"I heard there'd been an accident, but I can't believe this," George said when they rejoined Ned. "I had no idea it was so bad. It looks like the thing exploded."

"Ned can tell you about it," Nancy suggested. "I want to interview some of the people who witnessed the avalanche while it's still fresh in their minds."

Ned and George walked off. Ned pointed and talked, and George just shook her head.

Nancy talked to several witnesses—people who had been watching the sliders, vendors in nearby kiosks, and a few people who had been at the bottom of the staircase, waiting to climb up for a slide. But they weren't much help. No one had seen or heard anything that Nancy herself hadn't witnessed.

About thirty yards from the slide, she came upon the chestnut vendor. She helped him gather dozens of chestnuts from the snow. "My cart's a total loss," he told her. "But at least I'm okay—and the chestnuts. I can clean them up and salvage a little from this disaster, I guess."

"Did you see what happened?" Nancy asked.

"Nah, it hit me from behind," he said. "By the time I heard it coming, it rolled right over me. I've been selling chestnuts at the Carnival for thirty years. I've never seen one like this one so far. And this is only the second day. Warnings in the ice, howling werewolves, and now this. We never had a problem when one of the locals was in charge. Now we got this outsider—this Poodles guy."

"You don't think all those things are his fault," Nancy said. "Even the slide?"

"He's running the show, isn't he?" the vendor said. "Look, my wife is on the committee that hired this McNulty guy. Some on that committee didn't want him. He's got a reputation for 'pushing the envelope,' as they say—for going too far. Well, that seems to be just what's happening around here."

Nancy finished helping the chestnut vendor clean up and then returned to Ned and George. "I want to get closer to the slide," she told her friends. "Maybe we can piece together what happened."

She led George and Ned around to the back of what had been the slide. It was now just splintered, broken scaffolding, half buried in snow and ice. A small opening led into the wooden framework that formed the base for the slide. "Let's go in," she suggested. "But be careful. It probably isn't too stable at this point."

She pulled out her penlight, and Ned got a flashlight from his backpack. "Keep a light on the structure above us," she told him, pointing up. Scaffolding rose upward for two stories. "Watch for cracks in the wood. We don't want this framework to slam down on us."

It was grayish blue up at the top of the scaffolding. "No talking," Nancy whispered. "That's the top of the slide, and there's still a lot of snow packed up there. Loud noise can cause avalanches, and there's enough snow left to do more damage. If any of us hears anything strange, we grab the other two and all get out to safety, okay?"

George and Ned nodded, and Nancy stepped into the open framework. It was like walking into a two-story house that someone had just started to build. Hundreds of pieces of wood, some vertical and some horizontal, had been nailed together and crisscrossed to support the snow and ice above.

Nancy's penlight gave off just enough light to show them the way without glaring back too brightly against the snow that was packed on the ground. Ned kept his own flashlight beam up on the scaffolding, watching for cracks or places where a two-by-four had splintered and broken away.

Nancy cautiously tiptoed along, avoiding the footprints in the snow in front of her. *Someone has been in here before us,* she noted silently.

Eventually, the three of them came to the end of the path. They had reached the area underneath the long diagonal slide itself. It was really dark at this point. Wood beams slanted toward the ground, supporting the ice and snow that still remained after the avalanche. Nancy could hear the wind on the other side of the wall they had reached. Every time the wind whistled, what was left of the slide would creak.

When she heard the creaking, she felt as if an icy waterfall was trickling down her spine. "It's too dangerous to poke around in here," she whispered. "Let's get out."

She motioned for Ned to lead them back out through the framework. Ned and George hurried along, but Nancy moved more slowly. She paused often to examine the ground more closely and then the wooden poles around her. She was looking for something—anything—that could give her a clue to what had happened.

She realized that Ned and George were no longer in sight ahead of her. *They're probably already back outside,* she told herself. *Sounds like a good idea to me.* As she neared the opening, Nancy swung her penlight beam back and forth across the ground. Her cheek felt a sudden chill, and she put her gloved palm against it. When she took her glove away, the palm was damp.

She patted her cheek again as a small clump of snow plopped past her and onto the ground. Then another glob landed on her shoulder.

She looked up and another small puff of snow landed on her cheek. She knew she was under the top of what was left of the snowslide. It was dim up there—hard to see what was up above. She waved her penlight around, but its beam just didn't travel that far up. She heard an odd sound and thought she saw something moving on the wood crossbar above her.

Suddenly she heard a long, drawn-out creaking noise that grew louder and louder. She took a gigantic step toward the opening to the outside, but she didn't make it.

She looked up just in time to see a small wall of snow plunge down from the top of the rickety structure. In the split second before the snow reached her, she saw someone standing at the top of the framework. Then the smothering blue-gray cold buried her.

8

In the Light of the Full Moon

For a moment she felt paralyzed. She couldn't move her arms or legs. Only the top of her head peeked out from the mass of snow that engulfed her. Even though the lower part of her face was completely covered by the pile, Nancy instinctively tried to take a breath. She gulped in wads of snow that froze the inside of her nose and burned her mouth.

Her arms felt strapped down by the weight of the snow, but she knew not to panic. She forced her head to move from side to side and her shoulders up and down. She moved only tiny distances at first, and then inches. She kept pushing, each time moving a little more snow out of her way, until she freed her upper body enough to yell for help.

"Nancy! Nancy!" Ned's voice seemed to warm her

and give her a spurt of extra strength.

"Over here," she called out. "Hurry!"

George and Ned both rushed to help her. "I'm so glad we didn't wander off," Ned said. "We were right outside the door when the snow just rushed down." All the time he was talking he and George were pushing the snow away from Nancy.

"I haven't been here too long," Nancy told them. "But long enough."

While her friends worked to rescue her she told them about seeing the person up on the scaffolding just before the snow buried her. When her arms were finally released she was able to help with her legs. Finally the three emerged into the late afternoon sun.

"I'm going to find Jax," Ned announced, hurrying off to the area where the ambulances were parked.

"And I'll get you something hot to drink," George offered.

In just that short time she had been confined by the snow Nancy's physical strength had been sapped. Her legs felt shaky, so she stumbled over to a log and sat down. Ned rushed back, followed closely by Jax Dashell.

"Ned tells me you had your own private avalanche," Detective Dashell said. "And it sounds like it was no accident."

Nancy told him what she'd seen. "I saw someone

74

up there, but I couldn't identify him. He's probably long gone by now," she concluded. "What about the real avalanche?" she asked. "Was there anything suspicious about it? Have you come up with anything from your witness interviews?"

"Not really," Detective Dashell answered. "How about you?"

"Nothing," Nancy said. "But I'm sure that what happened just now wasn't an accident."

"Do you think you need to see a medic?" Ned asked. "There are still some over there." He tilted his chin toward the remaining ambulance. "They could check you out."

"There's nothing wrong with me," Nancy said. "I wasn't buried long enough to get hypothermia. I'm just cold." She took the mocha latte that George handed to her. "This will definitely help. I lost my last one."

"If you're sure you don't need me any more right now, I'm going over to talk to Poodles," Ned said. "I want to see if there's anything more I can do to help with the cleanup."

"That's cool," Nancy said. "I'll be fine." She took a sip of her latte and turned to Detective Dashell. "This is off the subject," she said, "but I saw Philip LeRoy on TV yesterday with the administrator of WildWolf. LeRoy said that wolves had escaped before and attacked his sheep. Did he ever file an official report about that?"

"I'm not sure," Detective Dashell said. "I'll check and let you know. Meanwhile, I'm going up to take a look at the top of the slide. I'll see you all later."

"I need to get home and change clothes," Nancy said. "These feel wet and sticky."

"I'll go with you," George said. "We finally got the Crystal Palace lighting program back up to speed, so I'm off for the rest of the day. I feel like I've been locked up in the lighting booth for days. It'll feel good to get away from this place for a while."

"Were you talking about the Crystal Palace lights?" Ned asked, rejoining them. "I just talked to Poodles. He's canceling most of the activities scheduled here for this evening. They need to get some major earthmovers in here to clean up this mess."

"What about the sporting events?" Nancy asked. "Most of those are at other venues—out on the lake or at one of the courses or fields. George and I are signed up for the cross-country race this evening."

"Most of those are still on—including the cross-country," Ned answered. "I've signed on to stay and help with the cleanup."

"Okay." Nancy nodded.

"Talk to you later tonight," Ned said as he left to meet the cleanup crew. "One of you better win that race."

Nancy finished her latte and dropped the cup in the trashcan. It almost seemed like a silly thing to do, since the ground was covered with litter and debris. She and George then stopped at the Heat Hut to talk to Bess for a few minutes. She had heard about the avalanche, of course, because a steady stream of distressed witnesses and shocked victims had descended on the Heat Hut. Bess had decided to stay on past her shift to pass out hot chocolate and coffee.

Nancy told Bess and George about her discoveries in Philip LeRoy's truck, and showed them the clumps of hair.

"Nancy, if that's wolf hair, LeRoy must have stolen the wolves," Bess said. She talked very fast as she began to put two and two together. "What do you suppose he did with them? I hope he didn't hurt them. Do you think he let them go? Or maybe they really did escape, and he caught them going after his sheep. That would be horrible for WildWolf. Wait a minute—if he found them with his sheep, he would have called the police. Or at least put together a press conference!"

"Whoa!" George cried, putting her hand up to stop her cousin. "Like you said at the beginning—*if* it's wolf hair. We don't even know that yet."

"Right," Nancy agreed. "I told Brianda to set up another meeting with Markie so I can show the hair to her. She'll probably be able to tell us right away what it is."

"You're right, you're right," Bess said. Her blue eyes squinted when she grinned. "If there's anything we've learned from working on cases with Nancy, it's to get the facts first."

"It's about five o'clock. George and I are leaving right now," Nancy told Bess, returning her smile. "We're going to stop at the college and drop off this new batch of grain mixture at the lab. I want them to cross-check the stuff from LeRoy's truck with the samples I found at WildWolf. Then we'll go change clothes and get ready for the cross-country race."

"I forgot that's tonight," Bess said. "Good luck." A small crowd of people walked in. Nancy recognized them as some of the rescue volunteers.

"Looks like we're going to be busy for a while," Bess said. "I'd better get back to work. Talk to you later."

Bess bustled back to the front of the room to take orders. Nancy and George stopped at the office tent to check Nancy out of her work shift. The coordinator there told them that Friday's schedule was still up in the air, so they should check by phone before coming in.

About half an hour later the girls left Riverside Park and the Carnival grounds. After a stop at the college chemistry lab, Nancy drove to George's house. While George cleaned up, Nancy called WildWolf and talked to Brianda.

"Some people phoned in leads," Brianda said

when Nancy asked about the missing wolves. "But no one's found a real trace. Markie is so upset."

"Well, I might have found *just* that—a trace," Nancy said. She told Brianda about the clumps of hair. "I'm in the cross-country race, so I probably won't make it out there tonight," Nancy continued.

"Markie and Christopher won't be here tonight anyway," Brianda said. "They got a lead out near Westfield, and they left a little while ago. They may be there all night, searching. But she should be back tomorrow. Come out any time—just call first to make sure she's here. What about work tomorrow? When should I come in?"

"Work shifts might be weird tomorrow because they don't know how long it will take to clean up the avalanche and get the scaffolding all torn down safely. They're going to be plowing and moving large dump trucks in and out. If you don't hear from me tonight, I'll call early tomorrow morning."

Nancy talked for a few more minutes, trying to reassure Brianda. She hung up just as George emerged, dressed in her red ski suit and carrying her skis and poles. "I am *so* ready for this," George said. "Let's go!"

Nancy drove them to her own house. Hannah was relieved to see her. She had heard about the snow-slide avalanche, and was horrified about the additional attack on Nancy.

"Did I or did I not tell you to be careful?" Hannah said. This time her frown was not pretend, and she wasn't smiling.

Nancy put her arms around Hannah's shoulders in a sort of half-hug. "I'm just fine now, and I'll be extra careful from now on." It was a familiar and affectionate exchange between the two. "George and I are cross-country skiing in a little while. How about whipping up some of your famous pasta and shrimp while I shower? We could use some carbo-loading!"

By the time they finished eating it was seven thirty—almost time to report to the starting line. Nancy finished pulling on her white ski suit. She still felt a little chilled, so she threw a ski mask and scarf into her bag—and off they went.

There were a couple dozen people in the field. Nancy recognized some of them as being pretty good skiers, but she was sure that George could take them all. She looked over at George, who was giving her skis a final buffing. She was a real outdoors person, and Nancy was sure that being locked up for nearly two days in a cramped lighting booth had been really hard for her.

Nancy did a few warmup stretches and pulled on her green ski mask and scarf. Then, with a shudder, she shook off the final uneasiness lingering from her near-burial. As she snapped into her ski boots she realized that she was really looking forward to the

80

race. She was eager to get away from the city for a quiet evening in the snowy countryside. *A great place to think,* she thought. *And I've got a lot to think about.*

Everyone lined up, and for a moment there was nothing but the soft sound of skis sliding back and forth on the snow. The starting gun broke the mood, though, and suddenly the race was on.

Nancy loved nighttime cross-country skiing. She'd only done it once before, but she remembered it vividly. It had been an eerie event, but breathtakingly beautiful. This night lived up to her memory. The racers slipped across fields covered with a few feet of snow. The pristine white surface sparkled with thousands of diamond crystals in the bright light of the full moon.

The only sound she heard was the *swoosh, swoosh* of the skis and the occasional crack of a branch nearby laboring under a coating of ice.

George seemed to sail ahead of everyone. It was almost as if she were on wheels. Nancy knew she was using all that pent-up energy she had stored while working inside for so long.

Nancy quickly lost sight of George and didn't see her for the next hour and a half. Although there were skiers around her, she felt alone with her thoughts. When she finally reached the finish line she had finished in the middle of the pack. She was thrilled to see George standing in the winner's box, holding a trophy high for the photographers.

"Congratulations!" Nancy said when George finally joined her. "I knew you'd do it."

"That was the best," George said. "It felt so wonderful to be out there, didn't it?"

"It did," Nancy said. "I loved it."

"Let's not quit yet," George said. Nancy could see the exhilarated expression in George's eyes even though she was also wearing a ski mask. "I know a short cut back to the car. Let's skip the shuttle ride back and stay on our skis. We can take our time."

"Sounds good to me," Nancy said. It was a little before eleven, and clouds had begun to skitter across the sky, yellowy white in the moonlight. The two pushed off along George's shortcut.

As her skis skimmed along the top of the snow, Nancy's shadow bounced ahead and then disappeared again as the moon was swallowed by a passing cloud. She felt a sudden chill, as if the temperature had plunged ten more degrees. For a few moments it was very dark. Then the moon was free of cloud cover again, and light flooded the snowy field.

For a long while there was no sound except from the movement of their skis. They didn't even try to talk. Nancy wanted nothing to break the almost mystical snow silence. But something did . . . something horrible.

A familiar wail chilled her blood. It was very close by. Even George stopped cold. They stood for a minute, waiting for a repeat of the howl. But it was deadly quiet again.

Then, without warning, a hairy gray figure rushed from behind a tree and charged into George, knocking her hard to the ground.

9

Wild Weather at WildWolf

Nancy snapped out of her skis and rushed to where George grappled with the hairy figure. Nancy swung her ski pole at it, scoring a hit on its side. With a human-sounding yelp the figure rolled away and jumped to its feet. Then it raced across the field and out of sight.

"George! Are you all right?" Nancy knelt next to her friend, who was still lying in the snow.

"There's something wrong with my arm," George said, cradling her left arm in her right. "It got sort of bent back when he . . . it . . . whatever it was jumped me."

Nancy darted back to snap her skis on. Then she helped George up and fashioned her scarf into a sling for George's arm. Slowly, they skied the rest of the way to the car, with George using only one pole.

Nancy drove quickly to the medical center emergency room. While George was being X-rayed, she called Detective Dashell and told him what had happened. He knew the area where they'd skied and told her he'd go right out. They both agreed that the snow should yield plenty of footprints for tracking.

George was finally released. "She has a badly sprained shoulder," the doctor told Nancy. "But I tell you, those were nasty scratches on her back. She said she thought it was some kind of wild animal, so we might have to have her start rabies shots, just in case. We took some cultures, and we'll be back in touch."

Nancy stopped at the pharmacy to fill George's prescription and then delivered her home.

When she finally got to her own house, Nancy found her answering machine full of news. She listened to the messages as she got ready for bed. Brief messages fired out from Ned, Brianda, and her Carnival coordinator about the next day's schedule. The next message was from Bess, and she had obviously been in touch with everyone else.

"YES!" Bess's voice yelled from the worn-out tape. "Go George! I called her first to tell her that you guys were on the late news. George holding up that major trophy, and you cheering. So cool."

"Wait'll you hear what *wasn't* on the news," Nancy mumbled to the answering machine.

"There's still a lot of cleanup to do," Bess chirped. "So they're only holding the events that are away from the park for the first part of the day. They're doing the polar-bear plunge—Ned's helping with that. And they've set up a temporary Heat Hut near the river, so I'll be working there. They're also holding the ice-fishing competition, and the golf match and softball tournaments. George is third-base coach for the game."

Nancy collapsed onto the bed. "Then in the evening," Bess's voice continued, "everything should be back to normal in the Park again. They're going to do the Crystal Palace lighting and the whole deal. I talked to Brianda and she said to tell you that Markie is home, so come out to WildWolf as soon as you can. I'll see you at the Hut whenever you get to the Carnival."

The last message was from Jax Dashell. "I found the spot where George was hurt," he said. "One path of weird footprints led into and out of that spot, but the snow was smeared around so that there were no really clear prints. There were some pine branches lying around. I figure whoever it was used the branches like brooms to sweep away the prints. I took some photos that we'll blow up. That might help, but I can't promise anything. Oh—and LeRoy never made a complaint about wolves attacking his sheep."

"What was a werewolf doing in the country?" Nancy mumbled. "Willy *couldn't* be right, could he?" She fell asleep before she answered herself.

On Friday morning Nancy woke up later than she'd wanted to—at about eight thirty. She checked her alarm clock and discovered she hadn't even set it. "Today I get some answers," she announced to the empty room.

Before she even got out of bed she called George. "I know Bess called you, so you should know everything that I know about today's plans. How do you feel? Do you need anything?"

"Nah, I'm okay," George said. "This isn't the first sprain I've gotten—and it won't be the last. I hope it will be the only one caused by a werewolf, though. Have you heard from Detective Dashell yet? What *did* happen last night?"

"We don't know yet." Nancy told her about Jax Dashell's call. "I'm going out to WildWolf this morning to have Markie take a look at that hair. I'll let you know what I find out. It's going to be hard to keep in touch by phone if you're out on a softball field though. Let's use Bess as our message center. Drop into the Heat Hut off and on and let her know what you're doing and where. I'll do the same, and we can keep tabs on each other that way."

Nancy called Brianda to tell her she was on the

way. Then she showered, dressed, drank a protein smoothie, and grabbed a protein bar, then headed out to the wolf preserve.

As she drove, heavy, wet, fat snowflakes began falling. Then the wind picked up and swirled the snow around until finally the air seemed completely white.

"Perfect weather for the Polar Bear Plunge," Nancy murmured. "But good luck at third base, George."

Brianda greeted her at the WildWolf office door. She immediately took Nancy into the conference room and closed the door. Nancy could hear loud voices arguing from the main office across the reception area—even through the closed doors.

"Is that Markie and Christopher?" Nancy asked.

"Yep, and they've been going at it like this almost all morning."

"Does this happen often?" Nancy asked.

"It has been lately," Brianda said.

Nancy walked to the door and opened it a crack. The office was across the large reception area, and the door was closed. Nancy could hear their heated voices, but couldn't pick out many words.

"What are they arguing about?" Nancy whispered.

"This morning it was about procedures at Wild-Wolf again," Brianda said.

Nancy motioned to Brianda to stop talking. She

then slipped out of the conference room and tiptoed across the reception area. She stood outside the office door and listened to the argument.

"If *I* had gotten the position as director, we wouldn't be having these problems," Christopher said.

"But you didn't," Markie responded. "*I* did. And I deserved it. You work for me, so you'll do it my way."

"Someday you're going to be sorry you ever got this job," Christopher warned. Nancy heard his footsteps pounding toward the door, so she scurried back across the reception area and into the conference room.

She kept the door open a crack and watched Christopher storm out the front door.

"So he was considered for Markie's job too?" Nancy asked Brianda in a low voice.

"You got it," Brianda said. "In fact, I gather from Markie that the competition was pretty hot. I think Christopher has always resented Markie for beating him out."

Nancy heard the office door open. She opened the conference room and saw Markie standing at the window next to the front door.

"Hi, Markie," Nancy said. Brianda followed her out of the conference room.

"Oh, hi," Markie said. "I didn't realize you were here." Her large eyes blinked in a rim of tears. She looked back out the window. "It looks like a real storm is blowing in," she said. "I know we need to talk, Nancy, but Christopher is gathering up the other curators. If we're getting a storm, we have to go on rounds immediately and make sure everything's secure."

"Do you need any help?" Brianda asked.

"No, we've got a routine mapped out," Markie answered. "Nancy, I hate to ask since you came all the way out here, but could you hang out until we're finished? We could talk then."

"Absolutely," Nancy said.

"Good. Help yourself to coffee and anything else. I'll be back as soon as I can."

As soon as they saw the trucks and other vehicles take off, Nancy turned to Brianda. "I'm going to look around in the office," she said. "You don't have to join me if you'd rather not. You can just stand guard out here."

"Are you kidding?" Brianda said. "I'll do anything I can to help my cousin—even snoop into her business!"

The office was divided into two large rooms. The first had several desks and computer stations. The back room was Markie's personal office.

Nancy directed Brianda to go through Christopher's desk in the front office. "He probably wouldn't keep anything important out here, where it could be accessed by anyone," Nancy pointed out. "But we need to look through it just in case."

Nancy went into Markie's office. After a cursory look through desk drawers and file cabinets, she found what she was looking for: a cabinet with two locked file drawers. Using her lockpick, she opened it. First she found the employment contracts for both Markie and Christopher.

"I'm not finding anything important," Brianda said. "What have you got?"

"Christopher's contract," Nancy said. "It says that if Markie leaves her position for any reason, he will be immediately named interim director until a permanent person can be found."

"Hey, that means that if she gets fired, he gets the job," Brianda said.

"Exactly. And it goes on to say that if the board finds his work satisfactory, he will be installed as permanent director, and they're not obligated to search any further to fill the job."

"So maybe he meant it when he warned her," Brianda said, her voice hushed. "Oh, Nancy, maybe *he's* causing the problems around here to make her look bad. Then she gets fired, and he's the alpha."

"Could be," Nancy said. "Hmmm, this might be something." She pulled a folder from the open drawer. "It's full of reports and letters from Christopher to the board of directors. They're all complaints about how Markie runs things at WildWolf. It looks like he's waged a systematic campaign against her."

"But this file is in her office, so she knows about it," Brianda pointed out.

"She sure does." Nancy laid out some letters on the desk. "Look at this. Every letter or report from Christopher has been answered by Markie."

"That must be why she's still got the job," Nancy said. "Apparently, she's satisfied the board that she's in control out here."

"So far," Brianda said. "Why does he even stay, I wonder? His plan clearly isn't working."

"If he wants Markie's job, he might think his best recourse is to stay here and keep chipping away at Markie's credibility," Nancy said. "In fact, maybe he's decided to step up the heat a little and cause a few problems that are not so easily explained away by Markie—such as wolves 'escaping' from WildWolf."

"Nancy, do you suppose . . . ," Brianda started. "Christopher could have kidnapped the wolves to make the board—and everyone else—think that Markie isn't capable of running a safe, secure animal preserve."

"It would be very easy for him to pull off," Nancy noted. "He knows how to handle the animals." She packed everything back into the appropriate folders and drawers and relocked the file cabinet. "I don't want to wait. I want to talk to Markie now."

"We can use my SUV," Brianda said. "They're making the rounds of all the enclosures and out-buildings. We're bound to find them."

The snow wasn't actually falling anymore. Driven by the hard wind, it was blowing horizontally, parallel to the ground, and was so thick that visibility was nearly zero.

When they got to the huge enclosure where the missing wolves had lived, it looked empty. Brianda explained that although no one could find any breach in the fence, they had moved the rest of the pack to another area in the preserve—just in case.

"I want to go in," Nancy said. "I haven't been inside yet. This is my only chance to look for evidence here. If there was any that was missed by the others, it'll soon be blown away or buried."

By the time Nancy and Brianda got inside the second fence they were in a near whiteout. Nancy knew immediately that they needed to abandon their original plan and retreat to the warmth and safety of shelter. The snow was now so thick that she couldn't even see Brianda, even though she was standing just a few yards away.

"Brianda," Nancy called. "We've got to leave. Come on." She heard Brianda's answer through the howling wind and looked in the direction of her friend's voice.

Just then she had that spooky feeling that she was

being stared at from behind. Nancy turned and saw two yellow eyes glinting at her through the blowing whiteness. Her pulse pumped as fast as the snow pelting her cheek. She was looking into the yellow eyes of one of WildWolf's famous residents.

10

A Blizzard of Clues

The wolf stared at her, and Nancy immediately diverted her gaze to its nose. She racked her brain for all the wolf behavior knowledge she'd gained from Markie. She knew that the wolf wouldn't attack them if they followed the rules.

She felt Brianda breathing next to her. "Brianda," she said. "Remember the rules." Then Nancy listed them off in a quiet voice.

"Stay alert. Stand your ground. No eye-to-eye staring contests. Don't give the wolf orders the way you would a dog. Don't turn your back on the wolf."

Nancy took a deep breath. "Okay, let's just back slowly out of here." She felt Brianda moving with her backward toward the gate. After a few minutes the wolf turned and trotted away into the snow. Still cautious, Nancy and Brianda continued backing up until they felt the gate behind them.

When they got back to the office, the others were already there.

"Brianda! Nancy!" Markie cried out when they arrived. "We saw Nancy's car still here, but not yours. We thought you'd gone off on some errand. I was worried about you out in this storm."

"It wasn't an errand," Brianda said. "We were looking for you . . . and we got caught in the wolf enclosure, which we *thought* was empty . . . and . . ." Brianda crumpled into a chair, shivering. A staff member got her a blanket and started a pot of tea.

"I don't understand," Markie said. She looked from Brianda to Nancy.

Nancy related their experience with the wolf. Markie and the others were horrified by the story. "Are you all right?" Markie asked Nancy and Brianda. "Are you sure you're all right?"

"Yes, we're fine," Nancy said. "But I would like to talk to you privately."

"Of course," Markie said. "But I need to find out what happened with those wolves." She looked around at the other employees. "What's going on here, gang?"

All of them looked at each other, shrugged their shoulders, and denied knowing anything about it. All of them but one.

"Christopher?" Markie asked. "Do you know something about this?"

"All right, all right," he bellowed, standing up. "I admit it. I put the remaining members of the pack back in the enclosure. I thought they'd feel more secure during the storm if they were in familiar territory. They're already unsettled, with Khayyam and Liz gone. It seemed to me that—"

"*Seemed* to you," Markie repeated. "That's always the problem! You do what 'seems to you,' rather than what I ask you to do. You know better than to move the pack without consulting with me first."

"You know what? I'm tired of consulting with you on every blasted little thing!" Christopher stomped toward the door. "As you Americans say, *I'm outta here*. You'll have my letter of resignation in one hour."

No one moved as Christopher's words echoed around the room. Everyone watched the door. It was like they were all waiting for him to pop back in, saying, "Kidding."

But after a few minutes, it was clear he wasn't coming back anytime soon. "Okay, everyone, I'm sorry about that scene—and all the others you've witnessed over the last few months," Markie said. "Let's just move on, okay?"

She walked to the window. "The visibility is still practically nil," she said, "but any of you who would

97

like the rest of the day off, please feel free. Those of you who don't want to risk the drive, you're welcome to stay until the weather clears, of course. Let's go fix some lunch. Nancy, if you can stay yet a little longer, you and I can eat privately and talk."

Several of the employees took off in SUVs or on cross-country skis, but a couple of them stayed. Nancy joined Markie, Brianda, and the others in the kitchen. Everyone pitched in to pull together a feast of leftovers—soup, sandwiches, and pie.

Nancy, Markie, and Brianda ate alone in the conference room.

"Brianda said you had something to show me," Markie said. "Something to do with my missing wolves?"

"First I'd like to talk to you about what's been happening out here," Nancy said. "I'm sorry that I overheard your argument with Christopher this morning. But I really couldn't help it."

"I know," Markie said, her mouth twisting into an expression of embarrassment. "Sorry about that."

"I'd like to know a little more about your working relationship with Christopher," Nancy said.

"Well, apparently it's over, for starters," Markie said. "It really hasn't been the best since we opened WildWolf."

"I told Nancy about Christopher competing with you for this job," Brianda admitted. Nancy felt sure that Brianda wouldn't tell her cousin that they had been going through her office files, though.

"Yes, it was pretty unpleasant at the time," Markie told them. "But I liked Christopher and admired his work. And I told him so. I really thought we had put the rivalry behind us and were both willing to work for the good of the preserve. Apparently, that was a stupid assumption."

"Do you think it's possible that Christopher stole the wolves?" Nancy asked. "Is he capable of releasing them into the wild?"

"But why would he do either of those things?"

"To sabotage you," Nancy said gently. "To get the board to fire you and perhaps put him in your place."

Markie was visibly distressed. "I never even thought of him," she answered. "I hate to think that would be possible. As much he might resent me, I truly believe he loves the wolves too much to endanger them."

"It's just an idea," Nancy said. "Think about it. Go back in your mind to the time around the disappearance. Right now, nearly everyone's a suspect."

Nancy reached into her pack and pulled out the tissues and placed them on the table. She opened them to reveal the hair that she had found in Philip LeRoy's truck.

"Where did you get this?" Markie asked, picking up a puff of hair and holding it gently in her palm.

"Do you recognize it?" Nancy asked, without telling her where it came from. "Is it wolf hair?"

"Not only is it wolf hair," Markie answered, "it's Olympia's."

"How can you be sure?" Brianda asked.

"Wolves lose their undercoat of hair in the spring," Markie explained. "It sticks to scratching posts, and it skips around the ground like tumbleweed. We gather it all up and store it in containers. Then we sell it to raise funds."

"Sell it?" Nancy repeated.

Markie stretched her arm across the table. "Feel my sleeve," she urged.

Nancy and Brianda patted the soft oatmeal-colored sweater. "It was knitted from the wolf 'wool' we gathered," Markie told them. "It's wonderful stuff. You can spin it like sheep's wool and then knit or crochet it. It's warm and snug, and really special to wear."

"And you're sure this is Olympia's hair?" Nancy insisted.

"Absolutely," Markie said. "Do you see these brown tips at the end of each gray strand? This is definitely Olympia's hair. We have a barrel of it."

"But Olympia isn't one of the missing wolves, right?" Nancy said.

"That's right. Olympia was born here, in fact," Markie answered. "She's never even been off the preserve. I just saw her when we made our rounds."

Nancy put down her mug of ginger tea and sat back in her chair. "What's the matter, Nancy?" Brianda asked. "You look surprised."

"Mmm, nothing," Nancy said. *How did Olympia's hair get on Philip LeRoy's truck?* she wondered.

A creaky noise like the winding of a spring interrupted Nancy's thoughts. She followed the sound to a large painted wood clock on the wall. It looked like a cuckoo clock. Instead of a bird coming out the little door, though, a wolf rode out on the little platform. And instead of twelve *cuck-oos,* they heard one long rolling howl with twelve beats: *Ahoo-oo-oo-oo-oo-oo-oo-oo-oo-oo-oo-oo.*

"Can you believe that clock?" Brianda said, shaking her head.

"It's pretty wacky," Markie agreed. "But one of our board members had it made for us in Germany. That's why it's in our conference room and not in my apartment."

"It got my attention," Nancy said. She went to the window and looked out. "The storm has thinned out a lot. I can even see a ray or two of sun trying to get out around the clouds. I really need to get back into town," she said.

"I'm not on until three o'clock, but I think I'll follow you in," Brianda said. "I'd like to see some of the games without being on call as a hostess."

"I'm coming in this evening myself," Markie said.

"I want to see the Crystal Palace. I hear they finally have it all ready to light tonight. If you ride in with Nancy, Bree, you can leave your car here and ride back with me tonight."

"Sounds good," Nancy said. She helped Markie take their lunch dishes back to the kitchen while Brianda changed clothes. Markie asked the other employees if they'd heard from Christopher, but no one had.

The storm had left its mark on the countryside. One of the WildWolf staff drove a plow just ahead of Nancy along the drive out of the preserve, making it easier for Nancy to drive on the road. She didn't have such a luxury when she got out to the country roads.

The snow had definitely stopped, and the sun was even peeking out. But the morning storm had made the road that led away from WildWolf nearly undrivable.

"I'm glad we left when we did," Nancy said. "It's going to be slow going." She dodged drifts higher than her car and used all her driving skills to stay on the road. It was so hard to tell where the road stopped and where the drifted ditches alongside it began.

The car swerved and slid, but Nancy maintained control. She stole a look at Brianda, whose face was white. "It's okay, Brianda," she said. "Don't be nervous."

Nancy wished she felt as calm as she tried to pretend she was. This was the slickest road she'd ever driven on—and she'd been on some really bad ones. She saw a small bridge ahead and knew it would be icy under the new snow. She did everything right as she approached the bridge, and she did everything right going over it.

But even her skill couldn't save them. Her heart seemed to sink into her stomach as she felt the tires skid across a snow-covered sheet of ice. "Hold on!" she said through clenched teeth as she felt the car leave the ice and sail through the air.

11

Frozen in Midair

Instinctively, Nancy turned the steering wheel—even though the car was still up in the air. The car came down on the other side of the bridge, on the left side of the road. She pumped the brake gently, so the car's momentum began to slow. The ice was too much of an obstacle, though. One last skid and the car finally stopped. Nancy's body slid into her door with a *thunk* as the left front wheel sank into a soft snowdrift.

Nancy and Brianda each took a deep breath. "You should patent that and make it a thrill ride at the Carnival," Brianda said with a giggle.

"Are you okay?" Nancy said, unfastening her seatbelt.

"I am," Brianda said. She sounded surprised.

"Good," Nancy said. "Now let's see if we can get out of this somehow." The left front corner of the car was buried so deep in the snow that Nancy couldn't open her door. Brianda got out first, and then Nancy climbed over the gearshift and went out the passenger door.

Nancy quickly got a shovel out of the trunk and began digging away at the snowdrift. After twenty minutes, Brianda took a turn. Nancy was about to call for help when she heard a welcoming sound in the distance. A vehicle was driving their way.

"It's Willy," Nancy said as the truck came closer. "He must have had a pickup or delivery out here."

Willy Dean's shipping service truck drove up behind them and stopped. Willy jumped out of the truck's cab and hurried over.

"Looks like you missed the runway a little, Nancy," he said, shaking his head. He got right to work hauling a large chain, a heavy cloth, and some rubber mats out of the back of his truck.

"I had a pickup near here," he told them. "Philip LeRoy's farm. Do you know he makes a private blend of sheep feed right there on that little farm? And he ships it all over the world. This batch is going to a ranch in Wyoming."

"Yes, I read that somewhere," Nancy said.

"Now you two ladies just stand out of the way," he told them. "I'll have this car out in no time. Hey, did you hear that the werewolf was sighted again last night?" he asked, walking to Nancy's car. His eyes widened as he talked, and his lip quivered a little. He seemed genuinely afraid.

"Philip said that a farmer friend of his saw the werewolf in one of his pastures," Willy continued. "Mind you, I don't mean one of those WildWolf animals, or just some big dog."

He padded the chain with the cloth so that it wouldn't scratch Nancy's car, then took the gridded rubber sheets and placed them tight behind Nancy's tires. "I told you, I've seen him myself. He looks like a wolf, sure . . . at first. But then, about the time you start realizing he's bigger than any wolf you ever saw . . . he stands up!"

He walked back from the snowdrift to where Nancy stood. "He stands up on both of those back legs and then he runs. He's sort of stooped over." Willy bent the top part of his body a little toward the front. "But he runs on those back legs. Just like a human being."

He walked toward his truck, then paused and looked back at Nancy and Brianda. "I've read a lot about those creatures," he said. "They look like animals, but they're not. They run like humans, but they're not. They're some sort of in-betweens—and they're dangerous." He climbed into the truck cab. "Well, let's get this puppy back on the road."

Willy backed his truck along the road and pulled Nancy's car out of the snowdrift and back onto level ground. She and Brianda gathered the rubber sheets from all over the snow and handed them to Willy. He disconnected the chain and the blanket and returned all the gear to the truck. Aside from a small dimple in the bumper, there was no damage to Nancy's car.

"Thank you so much," Nancy said as Willy climbed back up into his truck cab.

"My pleasure," Willy said. He gave her a big smile and cocked his head to one side. "I hope I didn't scare you with all that werewolf talk," he said. "I probably should just keep my mouth shut about it. No one believes me anyway."

"Well, I don't really think we have to worry about it," Nancy said.

"Okay," Willy said. "I'd better get this feed sent. I'll probably see you at the Carnival. I'm trying to get up the nerve for the Polar Bear Plunge."

He backed up and waited. As Nancy started to get into the car, Willy called out one last message from his open truck cab window.

"Just think about this," he yelled. "No one around here really knows Poodles McNulty. And no one ever saw a werewolf around here until he came to town. And no one has ever seen both Poodles and the werewolf at the same time."

"This has been one strange morning," Nancy said as Brianda climbed into the car. Nancy carefully pulled away.

Brianda spoke for the first time since Willy had driven up. "Nancy, do you believe in werewolves at all?" she said quietly.

"No, I really don't."

"Well, I didn't either—until this week," Brianda said. "Now I'm not so sure. Do you think Willy really thinks Poodles McNulty is a werewolf?"

"Sounds like it," Nancy said, chuckling. "I don't know—I sure can't picture that."

Brianda joined in the laughter. It was a great way to release tension.

Nancy stopped at the college and talked with the chemist. Her suspicions were confirmed. All the samples of the grainy mixture from LeRoy's truck matched all those from WildWolf.

When she got back to the car she told Brianda about the results. "I finally have some ammunition for Detective Dashell," she concluded. Armed with the reports she drove to the Muskoka River, site of several Carnival events. It was three o'clock.

The rest of the afternoon passed quickly. Nancy and Brianda joined the crowd that was watching the Polar Bear Plunge. It was a crazy event. Several people, some in bathing suits, some in regular clothes, jumped into the freezing cold Muskoka.

Medics stood by in case any hearts actually stopped. None ever did, although a spectator might have expected it from all the screaming and yowling that went on. Willy Dean chickened out, but Ned jumped right into the frigid river for all of thirty seconds.

People who strolled over from the main Carnival venue brought good news. The snowslide mess was cleared. Everyone began buzzing about what a great evening it was going to be.

George showed up after the softball game to tell Nancy that the threats carved into the Crystal Palace had been filled and smoothed away. At six o'clock the lighting of the Crystal Palace would begin the Friday Night Extravaganza.

The Extravaganza promised something for everyone. There would be ice dancing on Wawasee Cove, complete with a live swing band. The individual ice carving competition would be held in front of the Crystal Palace. And a rock group would turn up the heat along the banks of the Muskoka.

Nancy told Ned and George about the chemist's reports. "I'm going to find Detective Dashell and tell him," she said. "And I have to see what time you and I need to report for work, Brianda. How about the rest of you? What are your schedules?"

"I'm off until the Palace lighting," Ned reported.

"I'm off until then too," George said. "Even with my arm in a sling, I'll be able to help with the show."

"Great," Nancy said. She motioned to the temporary Heat Hut on the riverbank. "Somebody should check with Bess and see if she's working tonight."

Nancy checked in with her coordinator, who told her that there were so many changes in the schedule that she hadn't been able to contact all the volunteers affected. She had posted a couple of people at the gate to pass out flyers about the changes.

"Just wing it from now on," the coordinator told Nancy. "Your team has done a great job so far. A huge crowd's predicted for this evening. Do the best you can to keep in touch with your team."

Nancy set out immediately to find Jax Dashell. It didn't take long. She told him about collecting the two sets of samples and the wolf hair, and then showed him the reports.

"This is pretty convincing," the officer said.

"None of this really proves he had anything to do with the missing wolves," Nancy pointed out. "But it does seem to indicate that he has at least been to WildWolf, which he denied in the television interview. It is circumstantial evidence, but the exact custom-mixed grain that was on his truck was also on the preserve. And hair from WildWolf was on his truck, too."

"Well, there's enough here to at least question Mr. LeRoy," Detective Dashell said, folding the reports and putting them inside his jacket.

"I've seen him at the Carnival," Nancy alerted the officer. "He might show up here again."

Detective Dashell handed her a card. "Here's my cell phone number," he said. "If you see him, call me. Don't try to talk to him yourself."

Nancy agreed and the officer walked away. Nancy took a minute to enter his phone number into her own cell phone and then put it on her automatic dialing list. That way she only had to press the number 9 to dial the rest of the number.

Next Nancy went on her rounds and looked for her team. She walked around one of the spectacular iced-up fountains, its gushing water temporarily frozen in midair. As she came around to the back she heard a familiar voice.

"What's going on, Miss Drew?" Philip LeRoy asked. His tone was belligerent, and he seemed ready for a fight. He stepped in her path, freezing her just like the fountain water.

"Excuse me, Mr. LeRoy," she said. "I'm working, and I don't have time for a break right now."

"Oh, you're working all right," he said, his face twisted into a sarcastic sneer. "Working to get me in trouble."

Nancy's eyes darted from side to side. They were standing in a sort of alley behind the fountain. To their left was the rest of the alley, which seemed to lead to a dead end against a wall. To their right was

111

the fountain, which was so big that it hid them from view. She wasn't in a good spot.

Nancy took a breath and focused her thoughts. "I don't know what you're talking about, Mr. LeRoy. If you'll excuse me . . ." She started to turn and reverse her path, but he darted around and blocked her again.

"I thought I made my point the morning I locked you in my barn," he spat. "Now I find out that I wasn't completely clear. Someone saw you inspecting my truck at the softball game."

"Whoever told you that was mistaken."

"I might believe you," he said, "if I hadn't found out who you are. I've been checking you out." He put his hand in his pocket, and Nancy went on high alert. Every cell in her body was tuned to every move he made, every word he said.

"And what did I find?" He pulled his hand out of his pocket. Nancy flinched, but he held only a piece of paper. "You're a private detective."

"I'm telling you you're mistaken," she said firmly. "Now let me by."

Philip LeRoy stepped closer, completely blocking her from moving away. "This conversation is not over," he warned.

12

When Wolves Fly

Nancy's adrenaline zapped through her, and she felt herself switch to "flight or fight" mode. But she was trapped, so flight wasn't possible.

She casually dropped her hand—the one holding her cell phone—behind her back. While LeRoy rambled on, she flipped open her phone. With her thumb she counted along the buttons until she reached button 9, the number she had assigned to automatically dial Detective Dashell's cell phone.

She pushed the 9 button, then the CONNECT button. *Come on, Jax,* she thought to herself.

"So did you find anything interesting on my truck?" LeRoy demanded.

"I found wolf hair," she said. LeRoy teetered a

little and stepped back. "And I found samples of one of your grain recipes at WildWolf," she added. He seemed shocked and said nothing for a moment.

"Wolf hair!" he finally sputtered. "That's impossible."

"I'm afraid it isn't," Nancy replied.

"Maybe it was yanked from one of the wolves that attacked my sheep," he said defensively.

"The hair was gathered from natural shedding and had been cleaned to sell," Nancy said. "It was *not* pulled out. I think you lied about the wolf attacks—you never reported them. Did you steal the two wolves from the preserve?"

LeRoy's face flushed from its usual rosy red to a purplish hue. "What? You must be crazy!" he blustered. "Maybe I lied about the sheep attacks, and maybe I didn't. If I did it's because I know it's only a matter of time before it *does* happen. And I'm going to get that place closed—"

"What place, Mr. LeRoy?" Detective Dashell's welcome voice demanded from behind Nancy. She took a deep breath.

"I suggest we excuse Miss Drew and have a private conversation," Detective Dashell said. He nodded at Nancy who walked around LeRoy and a few yards past. She stopped when she was a safe distance away so she could hear the rest of the exchange between the two men.

"You have two choices, Mr. LeRoy," the officer continued. "You may accompany me voluntarily to the police station to make a statement and answer some questions, or you can be arrested for harassing Nancy."

Nancy couldn't see LeRoy's expression clearly, but she heard him gasp. After a few moments, he spoke. "I'll go with you," he said. "And I'll be happy to tell you a few things about that WildWolf and why it should be shut down. But you *won't* hear me confess to taking those animals."

Detective Dashell nodded at Nancy and escorted Philip LeRoy away from the frozen fountain.

Nancy finished her rounds, talking to the hosts she ran into. Then she stopped by the fortune-teller's cabin. She wanted to see whether the woman remembered any more about the man who had impersonated her. The door was locked, though, with a CLOSED sign on the front. By five thirty she was more than ready for refreshment at the Heat Hut.

When she walked in, Bess and George hurried to greet her. "I thought you'd never get here," Bess said. "George and Brianda told me everything that's happened. Here I am, stuck in this place, and you're out getting attacked by werewolves and real wolves and having all kinds of excitement!"

"Yes, well . . . some of it I could have done without—including the recent *human* attack." She told her friends about her impromptu meeting with Philip LeRoy.

"Oh, I hope he confesses," Bess said. "And tells them where the wolves are so they can be returned to WildWolf."

"Ever the optimist," George said with a disbelieving tone, but she gave her cousin an affectionate smile. Nancy and her two best friends walked back to George's table.

"And that would leave only the case of the werewolf," Bess said as Nancy and George took seats. "That needs to get solved really soon because it's starting to give me nightmares. I'll get you a latte," she said to Nancy.

"How is your arm holding up?" Nancy asked George as Bess walked to the counter.

"It's okay," George said, gingerly moving her injured shoulder. "I haven't had to take any of the pain medication the doctor gave me."

"Excellent. Did you have a chance to check with the others? How does everyone's schedule for this evening look?" Nancy asked.

"Bess is off at six for the rest of the evening," George told her. "Ned is going to be at the Crystal Palace at six o'clock for the ice-carving competition, but he's free after that. Brianda's schedule is pretty much up to you, I guess. We're all meeting at Uncle

Bud's at six o'clock. That's in about fifteen minutes. We might as well wait for Bess."

Bess brought Nancy's drink and hurried back to spend her last several minutes of the shift taking care of the people lined up at the counter.

At six o'clock Bess signed out, and she, Nancy, and George walked to Uncle Bud's Pizza—another famous River Heights restaurant that had opened a heated tent at the Carnival. Brianda was already there. Ned strolled in a few minutes later.

The five of them placed their orders, and then Nancy caught up Ned and Brianda on the latest news about Philip LeRoy.

"Hey, looks like the field has narrowed," Ned said. "For a while there were so many incidents and so many suspects, I didn't know who might be doing what."

"Wow," Brianda said. "I hope this is the end of it. At first I was sure LeRoy was the one who either stole or released the wolves. But then I switched to Christopher Warfield. Now I'm thinking it *was* LeRoy after all."

"Pretty weird story about Christopher Warfield," George said to Nancy. "Brianda told us about that scene. What do you think about it?"

"I'm not ready to rule him out yet, in spite of the evidence implicating Philip LeRoy," Nancy said. "Christopher has a motive, and the best opportunity of anyone. Plus he's the only suspect who we know is able to handle wolves."

"I still think that Poodles McNulty carved the message in the Crystal Palace wall," George said. "Remember how he acted? He was totally pumped about all the controversy. He even said he thought that wolves running loose would be good for Carnival business. That woman you told us about on the hiring committee predicted he might go too far to juice up the Carnival publicity. How do we know that he's not involved in all this somehow?"

"He *did* say he was going to put the River Heights Holiday Winter Carnival on the map," Ned added.

"Is no one but me worried about this whole werewolf deal?" Bess anxiously asked the group. She pulled a piece of pizza from the platter. The strands of cheese connecting it to the next piece stretched longer and longer as she pulled. "I want someone to tell me what that's all about."

"I'll bet Poodles hired an actor to play the werewolf just to capitalize on the missing wolf story," George pointed out.

"Willy Dean thinks it's more than that," Ned said. "He thinks there's a real werewolf."

"Brianda and I have an update on that story," Nancy said. "Willy thinks Poodles *IS* the werewolf."

"Well, I hope Poodles is just as much a showman as everyone thinks, and that the first story is the right one—it's an actor *playing* a werewolf," Bess said.

"Of course it is," George said. "What, do you think werewolves are *real* now?"

"Hey, you're the one who was attacked by one," Bess fired back. "You tell us!"

"Well, we have to admit one thing. We now know of four people—Willy, Nancy, George, and that farmer—who've seen this whatever-it-is when there was no crowd around to witness the sightings," Ned concluded. He gulped nearly half a glass of soda.

"There's one issue that no one's mentioned yet," Nancy said. She broke off a corner of a pizza wedge and popped it into her mouth.

Everyone looked at her expectantly. "Well?" Bess said. "What?"

"There seem to be *two* sets of crimes here—one set directed at WildWolf, and one set directed at the Carnival. Is this one case, or two? Are the two related? If so, how—and perhaps most importantly, why?"

After dinner Nancy and the others walked to the Crystal Palace to watch the ice-carving competition. The Palace was still in its canvas drape, awaiting the unveiling and light show after the competition.

Ice carving was one of the oldest Carnival traditions—a craft that was passed down through generations. Some used hammers and chisels and other sharp instruments; others used chainsaws. Willy

Dean used both. When the competition was over, Willy was the fourth person in his family to reign as champion for three years in a row. Ned led the others over to congratulate him while George went into the amphitheater's lighting booth.

"I see you recovered from your little accident this morning," Willy said to Nancy and Brianda.

"Thanks again," Nancy said. "This carving is really beautiful." They all admired the magnificent sculpture of an elephant carrying a sheaf of grass in its trunk. "It's so lifelike."

"Just a virtual version," he said. "I worked in the zoo for a couple of years before I saved enough money to open my shipping business. I used to—"

Willy was interrupted by a blare of trumpets. They all looked over to see Poodles McNulty ready to pull the cord and drop the drape that covered the Crystal Palace. The lighting was about to begin. The crowd gathered nearer.

With another fanfare Poodles pulled the cord, revealing the two-story, multitowered ice castle. George and her coworkers flipped a few switches, and thousands of lights turned on inside the Palace. Red, purple, blue, green, and gold lights flooded the elaborate structure and radiated through the ice, out into the frosty night.

A third fanfare sounded, but as the last note faded

away, a bloodcurdling howl rose up. Although Nancy had heard that sound twice before, it still was enough to make her jump. She felt as if all the blood had drained from her skin, leaving it as cold and clammy as the slush under her boots.

She looked up with the rest of the crowd to see the werewolf on the top of the Palace. More people gathered to watch.

"I told you he was real," Willy said, his face white with fear.

As with the previous appearance of this creature, half the crowd seemed frightened while the other half was delighted and cheering. Bess and Brianda huddled together, and Nancy felt Ned move a little closer to her.

George emerged from the lighting booth. She raced over to the ground spotlight that was trained on the roof of the palace. Wheeling it around with her good arm, she followed the beast with the light as it darted from tower to tower.

"Come on," Nancy said to Ned. She led him around to the back of the Palace. Leaning against the back wall of ice was a two-story ladder. "I thought so," Nancy said. "Looks like our werewolf came prepared for a getaway. Give me a hand." Ned helped her pull the ladder away just as the werewolf rushed to the edge of the roof.

The beast looked frantically down at them, his

glance darting from Nancy to Ned, and then back to Nancy again. He paced back and forth for a few seconds. Then, staring straight into Nancy's eyes, he leaped off the edge.

13

Let's Start Over

Nancy's heart vaulted into her throat when she saw the werewolf flying off the roof and sailing down toward her. She and Ned jumped back and skidded out of the way.

But they needn't have worried. The beast landed perfectly in a snowbank and then somersaulted out onto his feet. Ned dove toward the figure, but the werewolf hopped back and held his hands up in a defensive posture.

"Wait a minute," he said. "Wait! Don't be afraid. I'm not really a werewolf."

"I'm not afraid," Ned said. "I'm angry. I don't like anything flying at my girlfriend."

"Who are you?" Nancy asked. "And who hired you?"

"I'm Gabriel Winthrop," the man said, peeling off his wolf head. "I'm just a stuntman, doing a job. Poodles McNulty hired me to give the crowds a thrill."

"I knew it," George said, running up to join them.

"And you were hired only to perform here at the Carnival?" Nancy asked.

"Right," he said. "This Carnival is my only venue—I was hired to be on the bridge last night, and on the Palace tonight. That's all." His eyes shifted from Nancy to George. He was clearly nervous and uncomfortable.

"There have been rumors of a werewolf running around out in the country," Nancy said. "Several people have seen it. Was that you?"

A couple of security guards and a River Heights policewoman, along with Poodles, rushed up as Nancy asked the question.

"No way," said the stuntman. "I'd have to be crazy to be running around outside the city as a werewolf. Somebody'd probably shoot me." He looked at Poodles, and then back at Nancy.

"Are you okay?" Poodles asked Winthrop. "I almost lost it when you jumped off the building."

"Yeah, but—" Winthrop shrugged his shoulders. "I gotta tell them," he said to Poodles. He looked back at Nancy.

"Okay, it was me last night—out in the country," he confessed. "I was the one who crashed into you," he said to George. "I'm sorry. I never meant to hurt anyone. It was an accident, honest. I'll be glad to pay your medical bills."

"What were you doing out there?" Nancy asked.

"I had this gig," he said, "playing a werewolf at a party out at this hunting cabin. My car broke down on the way home. I knew I'd never get anyone to help me way out there late at night—especially dressed like this. I wasn't too far from home, so I decided to leave my car and just walk. I sure didn't think I'd run into you two out skiing."

"Wait a minute," Poodles said. His face was starting to flush, and he sounded angry. "You didn't tell me you ran into them."

"He sprained my shoulder!" George exclaimed.

"But I swear it was an accident," Winthrop said. "I heard you two, so I howled to scare you away. But you just kept coming, so I hid behind the tree. And then you came right toward me. I guess I panicked. I decided to make a run for it, and smashed right into you."

Poodles turned to Nancy, Ned, and the security people. "Look, he said he was sorry," Poodles said. "It sounds like it really *was* an accident. I'll make sure your medical bills are taken care of, George.

Gabriel really is a good guy. And you must admit, we sure added a touch of excitement to this event. That's what I was hired to do. I got the whole idea when I heard about the wolfnapping at that preserve."

"All right," George said, frowning and smiling at the same time. "At least I won't need rabies shots . . . I assume."

"Poodles, did you have anything to do with the missing wolves?" Nancy asked.

"Absolutely not!" Poodles said. "I had nothing to do with it whatsoever. And I'm sorry it happened. But as long as it did . . . it was a logical springboard for pumping some life into the River Heights Holiday Winter Carnival."

The security people and the policewoman talked briefly to Poodles and the stuntman. Since neither appeared to have done anything illegal, they all left.

"Let's go tell the others," Ned said.

"You go ahead," Nancy said. "I want to call Jax Dashell and see if he's made any progress with Philip LeRoy." She could hear Poodles speaking into a microphone at the front of the Palace. He was already introducing the stuntman to the crowd and whipping the onlookers into a frenzy of cheers and applause.

Ned walked around the Palace and Nancy hit the 9 on her cell phone. "I'm just calling to see what's happening with LeRoy," she told the officer when he answered.

"I questioned him pretty rigorously," Detective Dashell said. "He seemed shocked that anyone would suspect him of stealing the wolves. I kind of get the impression that he's afraid of the animals, so his having stolen them would probably be out of the question."

"I suppose," Nancy said. "What about the grain samples and the hair? How does he explain those?"

"He swears he's never even been to WildWolf, and he has a pretty good alibi for the night the wolves disappeared. He even offered to take a lie detector test on the spot."

"Do you suppose he's got an accomplice?" Nancy wondered. "Someone who does all the actual handling of the wolves?"

"I'm thinking that if LeRoy is involved, he definitely has to have someone else doing the dirty work," the detective answered.

"Okay," she said. "I suppose you've already heard what just happened out here."

"Yes, one of our officers called it in a few minutes ago. Let me guess—you're the 'young lady' who was at the foot of the Crystal Palace when the werewolf guy made his leap."

"You guessed it," Nancy confessed.

"I'm going to repeat my warning to be careful," Detective Dashell said before hanging up. His voice had a very serious tone. "This case isn't solved yet—not by a long shot."

Nancy went back around to the front of the Palace. A large crowd was milling around, admiring the gorgeous lighting effects and talking about Poodles's werewolf. Bess, George, Ned, and Brianda were waiting for her. Nancy repeated what the detective had told her about his interrogation of Philip LeRoy.

"I don't believe it," Brianda said. "All that trouble you went to, collecting the feed samples and the wolf hair . . ."

"The evidence still counts," Nancy pointed out. "If LeRoy is telling the truth and he didn't drop the grain or pick up the hair, someone else did. Either he has an accomplice or someone planted the evidence to implicate him."

The rest of the evening was nothing but fun for Nancy and her friends. They strapped on skates for an hour of spirited ice-dancing to swing music. Then they grabbed warm drinks and settled in for a couple of hours with the rock band on the riverbank.

They finally parted to head for their homes. George couldn't drive because of her arm, so she was riding with Bess. Nancy asked them to come by the next morning for breakfast. She wanted to take her car to the shop for a once-over after her accident. Bess could follow her and drive her from the body shop to the Carnival.

When Nancy finally got into bed she tossed and turned, working over all the clues in her mind. She was sure the answer was right in front of her if she could just get it into focus.

On Saturday morning Bess and George arrived for breakfast as planned. Nancy noticed that George seemed to be moving her injured arm more, although it was still in the sling. Over juice, scrambled eggs, and Hannah Gruen's melt-in-your-mouth cinnamon-apple scones, Nancy hardly talked. She was lost in the threads of thought she'd fallen asleep with. She knew that they could be untangled if she worked with just one thread at a time.

"Earth to Nancy, Earth to Nancy." Bess's words jolted Nancy out of her thoughts. The phone was ringing. She reached for the portable on the kitchen counter. It was Brianda, and she was in tears.

"Oh, Nancy, I'm so glad I got you. I have terrible news. Remember the four baby wolves you and the others played with last Tuesday when you came out for the Howl-o-rama?"

Nancy's stomach clenched with a pang. She could

still feel the warm, fluffy body of the wolf pup crawling up to her shoulder to nibble her hair and cry in her ear. "Yes," she answered, though she dreaded to hear what Brianda would say next.

"They're gone," Brianda said, her voice dropping to almost a whisper. "They've disappeared."

14

Howliday on Ice

"Oh, Brianda, I'm so sorry," Nancy said. "What happened, do you know?"

"They just vanished like Khayyam and Liz did," Brianda said. "And—"

"What happened?" Bess whispered. "Tell us."

Nancy motioned to Bess to wait, and focused on Brianda's voice.

"There are no clues that anyone can find," Brianda continued. "The babies are just gone. Apparently they were taken during the night."

"They wouldn't just wander off by themselves, would they?" Nancy asked

"Never," Brianda said. "Not at this age. Even if one was really precocious and adventurous, not all of them would be. We couldn't lose a whole litter at once unless something happened to them—something bad."

"Has anyone heard from Christopher?" Nancy asked.

"That was my next piece of news," Brianda said. "Christopher left River Heights the night he quit his job and returned to California—that's where he came from. He's called Markie a couple of times, and he was being very friendly. He even asked Markie for a job recommendation for someplace out there."

Brianda sighed, but it sounded a little like a sob. "Nancy," she said, "please help us find the babies—help us find *all* our missing wolves. Markie is trying to be very professional, organizing searches and working hard to figure out what happened. But she admitted to me last night that she doesn't have a clue. She's so depressed—it breaks my heart."

"I'll do everything I can," Nancy promised. As she put the phone back in its cradle on the counter, she felt more determined than ever to find the answers—*and* all of the missing wolves.

She told Bess and George why Brianda had called. "Not the babies," Bess said, her eyes wide. "Who would do such a thing? And *why*?"

Nancy was quiet for several minutes. Finally she spoke. "Let's start from the beginning of this case. Sometimes the best plan is to give up on the original idea and look at the problem from another perspective," she said. "Instead of trying to determine whether the motive behind the crimes is to close down WildWolf or to close down the Carnival, let's try something different."

"Like what?" George asked.

"Like, what if there's another motive altogether?" Nancy suggested. "For example, why would someone steal wolves from WildWolf?"

"For pets?" Bess asked. "Even though Markie says that's a bad idea? Hmm . . . maybe. Or maybe for their hides," she added with a shudder.

"Maybe to use as attack guard animals," George suggested in a hushed voice, "or even to hunt."

"Or maybe for *all* of those reasons," Nancy concluded. "Maybe someone wants to steal these prize animals to sell to anyone who can afford it. And they don't really care what they'll be used for."

Nancy bit into a scone. Her thoughts tumbled quickly as she added up the clues from the past five days. "Suppose the person wants to steal and sell the wolves, and caused all the incidents at the Carnival as distractions," she suggested. "It has to be someone who knows something about computer-driven theatrical lighting, and who knows about Philip LeRoy's homemade sheep feed *and* has access to it."

"But not LeRoy, right?" Bess asked.

"I'm not ruling him out completely," Nancy answered. "But it doesn't *have* to be him. And it

133

helps if the person is a skilled ice carver. Most of all, it has to be someone who knows something about animals—not only how to steal them, but also how to *ship* them, perhaps even illegally, to different points around the world."

"And since you—and even your friends—seem to have been targeted a few times, it has to be someone who knows you're on the case," George pointed out.

"A couple of these requirements fit some of our suspects," Nancy said. "But I can think of only one person around here who fits most of them. Bess, would you boot up my computer and see if you can get into the zoo database?"

"Sure," Bess said, jumping up. "What are we looking for?"

"Willy Dean said he worked at the zoo. I want to know everything you can get about his experience there," Nancy said. "George, could you call around town and see if you can locate a werewolf costume? If the costume shops don't have them, try some of the theaters or college theater departments."

While Bess and George got to work, Nancy called Ned and then Brianda and asked them to meet her in an hour at the Heat Hut.

"I got it," George called out from the living room, where she had used her cell phone. She returned to the kitchen, where Nancy was just finishing up her calls. "I found one at the Patches Costume Shoppe," she reported. "It's the same werewolf costume that Gabriel Winthrop used. It was turned back in yesterday and it's all cleaned up, ready to go."

Bess joined them with a printout from Nancy's computer. "Willy Dean was in charge of shipping at the zoo, and his job included sending animals around the globe," she read. "I also pulled up his bio and job history, and guess what? He spent four years in Chicago as an actor and lighting technician at a small theater!"

Nancy, Bess, and George stopped at Patches and picked up the werewolf costume, then drove to the Heat Hut. Nancy quickly brought Ned and Brianda up to speed.

"Are you going to call Detective Dashell?" Brianda asked.

"Not yet," Nancy answered. "I want to make sure we have the right man."

"How do we find that out?" Bess asked.

"We set a trap," Nancy said. "Last night when we were at Wawasee Cove, I poked around that old, abandoned ice-fishing shed down on the far end. It looked like it hadn't been used for years. It'll be perfect."

"So what's the plan?" Brianda said.

Nancy looked at her watch. "It's high noon," she announced. "We're going fishing—and I hope we catch a big one!" Nancy gave her friends their roles in her plan and then set it in motion.

Ned called Willy Dean. Ned and Nancy had rehearsed what he'd say, and the conversation went like clockwork.

"Hey Willy, I need to talk to you," Ned said. "I consider you my friend, and something's going on that I think you should know about. I figure if you have a heads-up on this, you can be ready to prove your innocence."

Ned held the phone receiver out a little. Nancy huddled with Ned so she could also hear.

There was a long pause. Finally, Willy spoke. "My innocence?" he said. "Innocence about what?"

"Look, I don't want to go over it on the phone," Ned said. "You know Nancy—I'm crazy about her, but she can really get caught up in this detective thing. She's got this idea that you're the guy who stole the wolves from the preserve. She also thinks you're behind some of the bad stuff that's been happening around the Carnival."

"You're kidding," Willy said. "What makes her think that?"

"I don't know exactly. She mentioned something about a fake fortune-teller and wolf hair. Oh, and she says she saw you try to bury her with all that snow under the superslide."

"Mmmmmmmm," Willy said. "That's going pretty far. Maybe I should talk to her."

"That might make things worse," Ned said. "You don't want her to think you're threatening her or anything like that. But I do know she's talking about going to the police with her theory. I don't want to sabotage her or anything, but I just think it's fair to let you know what she's planning."

"What are you suggesting?" Willy asked.

"I thought we could meet in an hour—maybe at the amphitheater. I know you and I know you'd never do anything like all this. I can tell you what she's thinking you've done, and that'll give you a chance to get your own evidence ready to prove she's wrong. But you have to promise you'll never tell her I talked to you."

"No problem," Willy said. "How soon is she planning on talking to the police?"

"Not until later today. She bought that abandoned ice-fishing shack on Wawasee Cove and wants to fix it up as a present for her Dad. He's out of town right now, and she wants to get it cleaned up before he gets back. So she's going to be out there from about one o'clock on. That's why I suggested you and I get together about then. She'll be so busy she won't notice I'm gone."

"Sounds good," Willy said. "I'll be there."

After Ned hung up the phone, Nancy went over the plan with her friends several more times. She knew that if she was right, Willy might get dangerous. She wanted to make sure all her backups were in place.

George, her arm still in a sling, went to the amphitheater to watch for Willy in case he *did* go there to meet Ned. But Nancy was sure he wouldn't.

Nancy, Bess, and Ned drove to Wawasee Cove. They went into the small shack on the ice and started setting it up. The shack consisted of four walls and a flat roof just sitting on ice a yard or two thick. There was no floor. What had once been a hole cut in the corner to fish into had long since filled in.

The only "furniture" in the small room was several wooden crates and one beat-up wooden chair. Nancy, Ned, and Bess stacked several crates and the chair in a corner and draped a painter's tarp over them. Ned, wearing the werewolf costume, crawled in under the tarp.

A hole in the roof had been cut to allow a stovepipe through. Fast-food wrappers and Styrofoam dishes littered the room. It was dark inside with the door closed, so Nancy lit the kerosene lantern she had brought. The smoke curled up through the hole in the roof.

She didn't have to wait long. She heard a car drive down the abandoned road leading to that end of the cove. Then she heard the car stop. Soon there was a short rap on the wooden door, and it opened without the visitor waiting for an answer.

"Well, it's you, Nancy," Willy Dean said. "I wondered who was in here. I thought this place was abandoned." He seemed very nervous.

"Well it was, but I bought it. It was really cheap and I'm going to give it to my father for a holiday gift. Do you know my friend Bess Marvin?" Nancy smiled at Bess.

"I've seen her around—hello. Aren't you a good daughter, Nancy," Willy said, sitting down on one of the crates. He was shaking. "I'm glad to find you here. I'd like to have a little talk."

"What about?"

"I understand you've been thinking I might have something to do with all the problems that have been going on around the Carnival," he said. "And even at WildWolf."

"Who told you that?" Nancy said.

"Never mind," Willy said. "I thought we'd have a little talk and get this all straightened out." He was breathing fast and seemed more nervous.

"We don't have to talk, Willy. I have proof, and I'm going to use it. And the police will be here shortly to receive it."

Willy jumped to his feet, knocking the crate into the old chair. "Well they're not going to find any of us here," he said. He reached out with his burly arm and grabbed Bess, yanking her over to the dark corner where he stood. Holding tightly to Bess, he pulled an ice pick from his back pocket and held the point against her side. "Now, let's go for a ride," he said to Nancy. "You drive. I've got some shipping crates that ought to fit you two perfectly."

"I've heard the werewolf uses this shack for his hideout," Nancy said without flinching. "Do you suppose that's true?"

Right on cue a horrifying howl pierced the cabin darkness, and the werewolf leaped out from under the tarp.

In the dim light from the kerosene lamp Nancy could see Willy turn as white as a ghost. He let go of Bess and fell backward, kicking the kerosene lamp into a pile of litter in the corner. A blaze surged up almost instantly, and the tiny room filled with acrid smoke and flames.

15

The Culprit Is Iced

Nancy grabbed the tarp and threw it on the fire. Bess helped stomp out the flames. Ned, dressed as the werewolf, opened the door to let out the smoke and stood guard, staring at Willy. Then he peeled off the full-head mask and signaled to Brianda, parked nearby, to call Jax Dashell.

"All right, all right," Willy said. "I see what's happening. You win. But get me out of here. I hurt my leg when I fell—I think I broke something."

Willy was still very white and shuddering. Nancy knew he shouldn't be lying on the ice, so she and Ned carefully eased him onto the tarp and dragged him off the ice and up onto shore. Once there, they wrapped him up in the cloth.

"The police and doctors are on their way," Nancy

assured him. Bess went to tell Brianda to call for an ambulance too.

"You stole the alpha wolves and the babies, didn't you?" Nancy asked Willy.

"I did," he admitted. "It took me years to set up an international black market network for those animals. And I was finally ready to make a little money on WildWolf."

"Your experience with the zoo helped," Nancy prompted.

"Yep. Not only to develop the contacts around the world. I also learned to tranquilize and capture animals without damaging the merchandise."

"But you didn't care what happened to them after they were sold," Bess charged. "How could you work with animals at a zoo and still not care about the abuse those wolves might get from your clients?"

Willy just shrugged. "I planned to pull off some pretty bold thefts during Carnival time," he said. It was like he was talking to himself now. "I figured they'd get less attention with all the hubbub this year."

He turned back to Nancy. "You know, you're not the only detective in this room. I did some major sleuthing of my own. For instance, I found from my snooping out there that Brianda was staying at Wild-Wolf. And, of course, I already knew your reputation as a detective. So when I saw you and Brianda hanging out, I figured you were working on the kid-napped wolves case."

"That's when you started following me?" Nancy asked.

"Well, first I tried to just get to know you—sort of be your friend." He smiled broadly. "I already knew Ned a little, so I figured I could keep tabs on you if we all sort of hung out together."

"You were the fake fortune-teller who gave us our fortunes, right?" Nancy guessed.

"Yes, I was," Willy said with a sigh. He related a scenario that was like the one Nancy had already guessed: that he had been following them and over-heard they were heading to the fortune-teller's. Then he just took advantage of the situation.

"It was perfect," he concluded. "I was able to slip you a fortune that matched the warning I had carved in the Crystal Palace wall."

"Why did you carve that message?" George asked.

"Again, I wanted all the talk around town to be about the Carnival," he answered. "I figured that would stir up the rumors and take the heat off the wolfnapping. I was especially proud of the lighting effect—blood red was a great idea."

Willy slumped into the tarp, then looked at Nancy. "I thought for sure that would discourage you—even scare you a little. I hadn't figured you out as well as I'd thought."

"What about the wolf hair in Philip LeRoy's truck?" Nancy asked. "And the bits of his custom sheep feed at WildWolf? Did you plant those to implicate LeRoy?"

"You *are* good," he answered, surprised. "Congratulations for pulling those clues together. Sure, I did that. LeRoy is paranoid about having the wolf preserve so close to his farm. He was an obvious suspect. It was easy to steal the samples from one of his shipments. I dropped the evidence at WildWolf when I kidnapped the first two wolves."

He wiped his sweating brow. Nancy could hear the sirens in the distance. "I spent quite a bit of time prowling around out there at night," Willy confessed. "I needed to get really familiar with the operation before I made my move. On one trip I noticed the barrel of wolf hair, and I pocketed some to plant around LeRoy's property."

"And the snow slide?" Nancy asked. "Was that an accident, or more of your handiwork?"

"I take full credit," he said proudly. "It was actually pretty easy. Just a few cuts with my chainsaw through strategic points in the scaffolding. Again— just a distraction from my *real* work."

"But how could you do that without getting caught?" Bess wondered.

"That was probably very easy," Nancy guessed. "In the weeks before the Carnival, chainsaws were the accessory of choice around the park. Dozens of workers were carving ice blocks, castle towers, and other sculptures around the area."

"You guessed it," Willy nodded. "No one looked twice at someone carrying a chainsaw around. When I saw you and your friends snooping under the slide after the avalanche, I decided it was time to remove you from the picture altogether. Too bad I wasn't successful," he muttered.

By this time Detective Dashell, his backup team, and the ambulance had arrived. The detective read Willy Dean his rights and arrested him while the emergency team treated him for shock and put his leg in a cast. Then they hoisted him onto a gurney.

"Before you leave, Willy, please tell us where the missing wolves are," Nancy urged. "It might even help your case with a jury."

For a minute he looked defiant. Then he seemed to lose the fighting spirit. "The babies are at my house," he said, "in the basement. The alphas are on their way to the Philippines, but they're probably still somewhere in the American West."

A relieved Brianda called Markie immediately and told her the news. After Willy was taken away, Detective Dashell escorted Nancy and Brianda to Willy's home to retrieve the wolf pups. Although they were evidence, Nancy and Brianda were allowed to take them immediately to WildWolf for holding until the trial. Detective Dashell also promised Brianda that he would do whatever it took to track down the alpha wolves.

When Nancy and Brianda got to WildWolf, Markie hugged Nancy and handed her a large gift-wrapped box.

"You didn't give her that crazy wolf-howl clock, I hope," Brianda said with a laugh.

"No," Markie said with a warm smile. "This is the only thing I could think of that would let you know how grateful we are, and how much this means to us," she told Nancy.

Nancy carefully unwrapped the package. When she lifted the lid, she gasped with delight. Inside lay a gorgeous wolf-hair sweater and matching cap.

That evening, under a midnight-blue sky with ice-crystal stars, Poodles McNulty held a special ceremony on the amphitheater stage next to the Crystal Palace. "We are all indebted to River Heights Holiday Winter Carnival employee Nancy Drew for cracking the wolf-napping case," Poodles told the huge crowd. "She has brought the wolf-napper to justice and closed the book on that scary period in River Heights history."

Poodles paused until the cheers died down, and then spoke again. "Nancy has told me that she had some help on this case, and I've asked her to introduce her team." He handed the microphone to Nancy.

"Thank you all very much," Nancy said. "Some of you might have been here when George Fayne turned the light on the werewolf on top of the Palace. Now it's her turn to be in the spotlight." George nodded her head briefly at the applauding crowd.

"And I'm sure you already know Bess Marvin," Nancy continued. "She's been one of those serving you warm treats in the Heat Hut. Well, she helped turn up the heat on the culprit, too." Bess smiled and waved.

"You've probably seen Ned Nickerson around the Carnival the last few days," Nancy said, taking Ned's hand. "He's had a lot of jobs, including helping with the snowslide cleanup. Yesterday he imitated a werewolf and helped catch a criminal." Ned bowed to the audience.

"Finally, you might have turned to Brianda Bunch for help finding your way around the Carnival," Nancy said, gesturing toward her friend. "She's been a hostess the last several days. I turned to her for help too—help on this case. And she stepped right in. Now that you all know the werewolf was a fake, consider a visit to see some real wolves at WildWolf, which is run by Brianda's cousin. It's a fascinating place." Brianda smiled and cocked her head shyly. The crowd cheered again as Nancy turned the mike back over to Poodles and returned to her friends.

"Did you ever notice the same thing I did?" Poodles crowed. "Every one of these young detectives is a Carnival employee." Poodles pumped his fist in the air. His face glowed with an expression of pride and enthusiasm as he worked the crowd into more cheers.

He looked at Nancy and motioned to an assistant to hand him some envelopes. "Nancy, the Carnival is especially thankful for your hard work. With the wolfnapping case solved, the people of River Heights and guests from around the world can really enjoy the rest of the Carnival. As a token of our appreciation, here are gift certificates for you, George, Bess, Ned, and Brianda. Take these to Albemarle's and redeem them for new skis and designer ski clothes with our thanks."

This time it was Nancy and her friends who cheered. "This is so cool," Bess whispered to Nancy as they all went up to collect their gifts. "I can't even think about what might have happened to the baby wolves if you hadn't solved this case, Nancy."

"Not only that," George added, "but she figured out what was going on here at the Carnival. And look at that crowd—this Carnival is going to have a record turnout."

"Hey, what did you expect?" Bess concluded. "With Nancy Drew on the case, the River Heights Holiday Winter Carnival was bound to be a *HOWL-ING* success!"